I0612117

In Each Moment

An Anthology of Short Stories
about Life & Love

Written by:
Michelle R. Yisrael

Published by I AM Media Books

In Each Moment © 2019 Michelle R. Yisrael

Cover Design by Yehudah Graphics
Editing by The Words Doctors
Interior Layout by Build-A-Book

ISBN: 9781951667009
Published by I AM Media Books, Michigan, USA
Media to Awaken the World!

www.iammediabooks.com

Table of Contents

1

In Need of Comfort

She suddenly felt uneasy. She passed the corner store and saw a tall slender man wearing a white turban. She guessed he was only a few years older than her Uncle Ray. She'd seen him before with the men dressed in white who preached, ...no screamed, at people on 87th Street at the Dan Ryan where she got on the train to go to Columbia College. Regularly, they stood on the corner screaming at people and asked if they knew who they were. They held Bibles in their hands, but she rarely saw them open and read from them and when they did, they shouted a bunch of reviling. Chasah wondered if the Bible's main function was to make people feel damned. She'd overheard her grandfather and uncles arguing about that same thing at every family gathering for the last two years. Uncle Ray never took the time anymore to talk to her about life and share the family stories, like he used to.

Uncle Ray was the first one to start the Bible argument and he wouldn't let up. He seemed to have an agenda and his agenda was to bring discord in this family. To her it seemed as though he came to the family gatherings just to pretend to be better than everybody else, because he now thought differently about his life. She heard her grandfather say Uncle Ray was being "righteous over much." Chasah Googled it. It came from the book of Ecclesiastes 7:16, "Be not righteous overmuch; neither make thyself over wise: why shouldest thou destroy thyself?" As she reflected upon the verse, she thought it meant for someone to be self-righteous and judgmental; thinking they are better or more righteous than others. Or being so righteous they forget to enjoy life, love the people around them, and be a good example of virtue and honor.

Chasah even heard Uncle Ray announce that he wouldn't eat the BBQ ribs anymore.

"That swine!" he'd call it.

So, whenever it was time to eat, Auntie Christa fixed him a plate of greens, potato salad, macaroni and cheese and chicken. He would never say chicken was *"that swine."* Chasah noticed he put the plate Auntie Christa gave him on any table and never came back to eat it. He was offensive and pushed his family away with his contentiousness. He even got mad if anyone called him Uncle Ray. He wanted everyone to call him Zebulun. Everybody seemed perplexed when he came to this new way of thinking and expected his entire family to walk in his shoes; nobody understood why. Their lack of understanding frustrated him and kept him in a constant state of anger. He didn't seem to have patience enough to get his point across. If causing your family to resent your presence was typical of this new way of thinking, Chasah decided she wanted no part of it. Ever!

This same man she saw at the corner store also passed her most evenings under the viaduct walking from the bus stop. She guessed he was coming from work since she never saw him carrying books. Her uncles warned her to be careful walking under that viaduct.

"You're a beauty Chasah," they warned. *"Many men won't know how to handle you. You will have to sift through the junk to get you a decent young man who will cherish and protect you. Don't you settle."*

Chasah was a true beauty to behold. She was well-formed with a striking hourglass figure; the essence of The Commodores' *"Brickhouse"*, turning the heads of men young and old as she strutted down the street unconscious of her own natural sensuality. It was a natural walk—she didn't have to practice. Each time she walked past a male with wanton eyes, she stiffened and awkwardly tried desperately to change the way she walked.

"She moves like a Maltese kitten," a security guard once whispered in the campus hallway.

They didn't know whether to watch her buttocks or her thick, rounded, sexy calves as she sauntered. She didn't walk, she sashayed. Her uncles said Chasah's mother moved the same way, before she aged and gained weight. She was well-balanced and agile. She had a stealthy stride, which made her buttocks twitch methodically, ever so gently, from one side to another with an innate simplicity. Her dresses were never too short, and it was evident she was taught to wear a slip under her dresses, unlike most young women these days. She made a conscious effort not to wear her dresses to short or her pants too tight. At any rate, watching her sensual stroll brought life to many a man on the street corner.

One year and six months after Chasah and Jake met during math class, things took a turn. He transferred to Columbia from Tuskegee in the fall term and they were in the same group in that math class. They enrolled in the statistics course together the last day of the fall semester, just before winter break. As she remembered it, they were supposed to meet up after her last literature class and go to Jake's house to spend time together. They hadn't seen each other, except in statistics class or study group, in more than two weeks. When they talked the night before, they were both excited about being on break for almost three weeks and looked forward to the possibility of spending time together.

She waited outside the theater until a security guard kept trying to talk to her. He made her uncomfortable with his advances. Chasah felt as though she needed protection from pushy men all the time. She waited outside at the front door until there were only five people remaining at the busy bus stop on the corner. *Could he have walked right past her?* She stood there so long she began to feel ashamed for waiting.

Finally, she decided to get on the next bus. She swiped her bus pass and attempted to walk down the aisle with a heavy bag on her shoulder. Jake would have helped with her bag. Suddenly, she felt a sneeze attack her in the middle of an attempt to pull the handicap seat down. The driver pulled off and she lost her balance. She grabbed the only thing she could to keep from falling, a man's arm. He stiffened, making his body strong and stable enough for her to get her bearings as she struggled to sit down. She had no apprehension in grabbing his arm and he didn't pull back. He had her back; he was her railing. As she settled into the seat, she thanked him. He simply nodded his head.

Her thoughts raced back to Jake. She wanted to get home so she could be there when he called.

"I knew I should have went back home to get my cell phone this morning," she whispered to herself.

Instead, Chasah chose to catch her train and get to class on time. She knew Jake was probably blowing up her phone by now. She didn't know how she missed him; she stood in the same spot she'd stood many times while she waited for him. He always came. She didn't need her cell phone before to catch up to him. There had been times when her phone was still in her bag and on silent, yet he found her. It never took this long. So, she was anxious to hear his explanation for standing her up.

Chasah waited for Jake's phone call for seven days. She dialed his number four times that week. The first time, there was no answer. The second time, no answer. Again, the third time. The fourth time she called, she got a busy signal. She fought with herself about dialing his cell again, she didn't like how it felt to be so clingy and possessive. She wondered if he was locked up, so she asked his friend Cory and he said he hadn't seen Jake either. It was common for young men to disappear for a time in the hood. Her mother would always get so angry when she drove around the city and saw the police demanding young brothers stretch their arms on the top of the car while being searched. Many times, it was for no apparent reason. Her own brother was stopped because of his locs all the time.

Jake told her not to come to his house unless he was expecting her, because his younger brother always had his friends over, who were known gangbangers. Jake's father was killed in the county jail when they were younger; and their mother was always at work. Chasah walked over there anyway, it was only a few blocks away. She did see his mother's car when she walked up, so she decided to ring the bell. His brother and friends were on the porch smoking blunts, even though it was cold outside. They heckled her as she approached the porch and wouldn't let her up the stairs.

Jake's brother quipped, *"What do you want? My brother ain't here."*

"Can I ring the bell to talk to your mom?" she begged.

"For what? I said he ain't here, you ain't gone be bothering my mama", his brother snapped angrily.

"I just wanted to ask her a question," Chasah responded.

"You ain't gone be asking my mama no questions. If Jake wanted to talk to you, he would have called you. Did you call his phone?" he taunted.

"Yes, but he's not answering," she responded sheepishly.

"Then I ain't got nothin to tell you either!" he said as he appeared to bark at her. *"If my brother wanted to talk to you girl, he would have called you."*

Chasah turned around confused and hurt.

Someone in their math study group picked up a flyer in the library about an event promoted by Sunshine Moxie Entertainment at the Exstacy Lounge on North Avenue and Dearborn. King

Corso was opening the pre-party show for Bigbellyrelli to celebrate the end of the semester, and Chasah wanted to make sure she was there. Everybody said they were going. They all bought tickets, including Jake. She had been in the house all week, since it was winter and cold outside. She had no place to go so she stayed inside and spent the week in her room reading. She thought Jake would be at the party too. She hoped he would. It was very unlike him to not call her. They usually talked on the phone for hours every evening, sometimes talking about nothing, sometimes talking about everything. Sometimes just holding up the line. Neither wanted to let the other go.

Chasah planned a therapeutic bath, because she thought it would calm the churning in her stomach, which disconcerted her thoughts since the last day of the semester. She deliberately soaked in the tub in preparation for the party. When the water cooled, she added more hot water. When the bubbles subsided, she added more bubble bath. She needed ambiance, so she turned off the lights and lit a Hawaiian scented candle. She washed every part of her body. Taking a long, hot bath comforted and made her feel good.

After her bath, she put powder and perfume on everywhere she could think of. She wanted to smell good. A long, relaxing bath and taking time to spruce herself up was an enjoyable practice she'd learn to neglect later in her life. She chose to wear a svelte red dress her auntie bought her as a birthday gift. She oiled, brushed, and curled her hair so it would sit on her head just so. She prided herself in her very large and well-kept natural hair. She loved her natural hair. She decided to wear a twist out because Jake liked it that way. She felt special because God made Black hair so strong and beautiful. She wondered why the Muslim girl she passed in the halls every Thursday kept her beautiful hair covered all the time. She didn't think God made their beautiful black hair to be tied up all the time. Like her sensuous walk, Chasah's natural hair turned many heads.

Chasah left home for the party feeling confident she looked and smelled good enough for someone to eat. She was certain Jake would be at the party, since the organizers were both their friends. She was ready to talk to Jake with the confidence of an innocent fawn grazing in the woods, unaware of the wolf approaching his prey at a snail's pace. She practiced what she'd say to Jake in the mirror. She couldn't wait to see his smiling face and give her ear to hear his reasons for standing her up and altering their carefully constructed plans.

Chasah and Jake liked Bigbellyrelli and King Corso. Bigbellyrelli gave his audience a nice balance between jazz, R & B and hip hop. He was her favorite. But it was really difficult to enjoy the show without Jake. Chasah danced until she was ready to drop. She danced with or without a partner. It didn't matter, she simply enjoyed dancing. She danced until her feet and legs felt numb. She loved to dance even that day, the disappointment of Jake not being there didn't stop her. She paid little attention to the latest dance craze. She just moved every part of her body to the music. She was always in sync. Music had always been in her bones. She should have learned to play an instrument. Music was soothing and relaxing to her. That night she didn't slow dance, she saved that for Jake.

Chasah wanted to get as close to Jake as she could. She wanted to lean on him, supported by his strong body and his big arms. She wanted to be comforted by both his touch and the music simultaneously. The anticipation of his touch made her dance even more. She kept her eyes on the door, waiting for Jake to enter. The party was nearly over before she realized, he was not coming. They were supposed to go to that party together. She went alone and he never showed. She wondered if he remembered. She wanted to talk to him, he had been her best friend since they first met a year and a half ago. She wanted to look into his kind eyes. Little did she know, she'd learn to live with that achy feeling, the pain of yearning for Jake. It was a pain she'd learn to hate and at the same time look forward to with anticipation.

Chasah just turned 19. She should never have gone to that party alone on public transportation. She was on her way home at midnight, alone. She should have called an Uber. To get from the bus stop to her house, she needed to walk about five blocks, pass under a long viaduct, and walk across a series of vacant lots. She usually walked that walk faster looking around her cautiously. She was usually conscious of every noise and jumped at every sound. That evening, she was distracted. She wasn't paying close attention to her surroundings. She was both exhausted from her night of excited dancing and somber, because she hadn't seen nor heard from Jake in a week. She kept her arms bundled tight, because of Chicago's winter chill.

As she approached the end of the viaduct on the way home, she heard footsteps behind her. The streets were deserted because of the cold and time of night. She turned her head slightly, to try to see who was walking behind her without breaking her own stride. She walked faster. He picked up his stride. She thought of running, but her feet were numb, and she had a difficult time picking them up quickly. Before she knew it, the footsteps caught up with her. Abruptly, there was an arm around her neck. A smelly skull cap was slid over her head covering her face. The perpetrator then put a knife to her throat. It seemed as if he did it all at the same time, in one smooth and swift swoop.   It seemed as if he had much skill and practice. She wondered how many other young girls were preyed on by him. There was no delay in the steps he took to secure Chasah as his prey.

He whispered in a fierce tone, *"Do what I tell you and you won't get killed. Scream or try to run, and I'll stick this knife in your neck."*

Chasah was petrified. She didn't make a sound. He pulled her over to the stairs where passengers came down from the Metra train. There was not a sole in eyesight or earshot, from what she could tell

"No!" whimpered Chasah

"Shut up!" he retorted. *"This is what happens to the daughters of Zion who are haughty and walk with stretched forth necks and wanton eyes. I see you walking and mincing as you go and*

making a tinkling with your feet. You don't cover yourself. What did you think was going to happen? You asked for it. Well, I'm giving it to you."

Her attacker timed it perfectly. While he performed his fiendish act, no train stopped at the station. She listened for a train. She paid close attention to his voice trying to remember it. He put his hand over her mouth, as his hips bounced up and down on her torso like an animal and pushed her back into the edge of the steps causing her more pain. Chasah knew Jake, as it was biblically coined. He had loved her tenderly for six months. He didn't enter her with such rough force. This was different, the assailant's poisonous rod invaded her hidden place hatefully. Tears rolled down her face, and she whimpered from the abuse.

"Shut up, you better dry up those tears, I ain't hurtin you, you ain't tight. You done this before, more than once. You're a bad girl!" he said gritting his teeth.

He moved the knife closer to her throat as he spoke. Chasah was afraid not to do what she was told and managed to suck up her tears.

"Move your hips damn it, you know how to do this!" Chasah moved her hips slowly as he humped.

"Damn you, move faster. I am almost there!" he snarled.
Chasah could feel the tip of the knife penetrate the skin in her neck. She recognized his voice, but she wasn't sure where she'd heard it.

"Please don't hurt me," cried Chasah. *"Please stop."* she wept.

"Kiss my neck," he moaned. She delicately rubbed her nose and checks on his neck and moved it around being careful not to let it touch her lips.

"Please stop!" sniveled Chasah.

"Shut up! Take it out and put it in my mouth," ordered the perpetrator as he gently jabbed at her breasts with the tip of his knife.

Chasah submitted unenthusiastically, took a deep breath and wept quietly.

"Bad girl, I told you to shut up and do what I tell you to do!" screeched the attacker. *"No! Don't*

try to use both hands," he corrected her as he stuck tip of his knife closer to her neck again. He pushed harder to pin one arm under her. He lifted the skull cap up just slightly under her nose.

"Open your mouth and kiss me now!" he groaned. *"I can make you feel good. You know you want it. I seen you walk,"* he murmured. *"I been watching you."*

"No, please!" Chasah sobbed.

"Don't let me tell you to shut up one more time. I told you to kiss me," he grumbled his final order before she heard his last deep groan and his venom spewed in her hidden place. He tightened his squeeze on her for what seemed like forever. Chasah felt her own hidden place pulsate and cascade as he squeezed her.

"Bad girl," he whispered.

Chasah's heart lamented low and deep, she was betrayed by her own body. She felt a deep shame. Indeed, she was a *bad girl*. She sighed.

Her attacker finished and got up quickly, *"Don't take that hat off your head until I tell you to."*

He ran off in the same direction from which he came. Chasah thought she heard his footsteps moving toward the gate. She laid there for a bit, until she couldn't feel his presence around her anymore. She was afraid get up, afraid to look after him. She got up after a few more minutes, pulled the skull cap off her face, looked around her slowly and deliberately, then ran home, despite the numbness in her feet and legs.

She tried to close her coat as she ran but noticed the buttons had been ripped off. Everything happened so fast, she didn't notice when he ripped her coat open. She didn't want anyone to find her torn panties and underwear, so she picked them up and stuffed them in her pocket. She had on one shoe and could not find the other.

It wasn't until she hurled herself into the door that she could feel the sting of his heavy brutal hand across her face, her bruised and throbbing lady parts, and the reminiscent aching from his fist in her stomach. Her mother jumped out of bed. She was finally able to scream loudly, enough to startle everyone in the house. Words finally poured out of her mouth. As Chasah told her mother what happened, she held her and rocked her. Her mother rarely hugged her.

Chasah felt safe and secure at home in her mother's embrace.

When the police came, they asked so many questions. According to them, she did everything wrong. She wondered how they would have reacted had it been them in her place. Their tone was accusatory. When she was taken to the hospital, she was examined. The doctor said the tear in her lady parts wasn't bad enough for stitches. Once the doctor discovered Chasah wasn't a virgin, he became as suspicious as the officers.

Chasah felt awful. She felt dirty. She felt it was her own fault. She couldn't identify her rapist, because she did not even try to get a look at him. Their voices were accusatory. They couldn't understand she did not want to see his face. She just wanted him to leave her alone. She just wanted the police and the doctor to leave her alone now as well. She didn't like their tone and the way they treated her. She didn't even like the way they questioned her mother in an interrogatory manner. Her father came to the hospital. He and her mother had not lived together since Chasah as a little girl. Her mother always called him when there was an emergency, and he always came.

No one knew, except her immediate family, that Chasah was violated because of the sensual stroll that came to her from the one who made her. No one could ever know how her lady parts betrayed her, that would be her secret forever. Unlike the memory of her Jake, this memory was like a poignant wound in the heart. Her youthful naivete was stolen, vanished forever after her rape.

That voice though, she wanted to remember. She listened for the fierce voice almost every day. For a long time, she wondered what would have happened if she had screamed or tried to run away. Maybe she could have gotten away. She remembered being frozen. Maybe her screams would have been heard by someone. She didn't know why she made it so easy for her rapist, that's what the police told her. She was just scared, too scared to do anything other than follow instructions. She felt sick and guilty when the police officer asked her several times why she didn't scream or at least try to run. She wondered why too. The thought of a knife stuck in her throat wouldn't allow her to do anything but what she did. She was powerless against his weapon, was her conclusion.

The voice she heard was not the voice of a teenager. It was not the arms of a little boy. He didn't feel like a largely built man, but he was a man just the same. Nobody except her mother and her uncle said she did the right thing. They both told her maybe had she not cooperated, she may not even be alive to tell her story and feel the comfort of the words they spoke to her.

She could still feel the bitter cold as she lay there under the brutal attack. She could still feel the aching of a broken and naïve heart stolen. Chasah was haunted by the fact she did as she was told. Unable to hold back her tears, she followed every order. She was petrified and feared her attacker would slit her throat. She did not know what else to do. She was sorry she even went to that party. She was even more sorry she went alone. It was the last time Chasah walked that walk alone. Five blocks. In the dark. From the bus stop. Under the viaduct. Past the series of vacant lots to where she lived.

Chasah remembers his voice even today. Several years later she heard that voice at the laundromat, as she pulled her head out of the dryer taking the clothes out. She didn't turn around. She made a beeline for the door, leaving all her family's laundry behind. She thought of nothing but getting out of there. Again, he had the advantage. She could recognize his voice, but she had no idea how he looked. Even now, as she ran out the door of the laundromat, she was afraid to look.

Chasah ran home and told her mother and uncle why she left the clothes at the laundry mat.

The two of them moved fast! They didn't seem upset. Her mother picked up the phone immediately and called the police. Her uncle took Chasah's hand and walked to the door, down the stairs, down the four blocks to the laundromat. When they got there, there was only a young woman and her children there washing clothes. The police took a long time to come. There was no sign of Chasah's attacker, just more questions, another useless police report, but thankfully no hospital and no probing like the day of the attack.

During the violation, her rapist pulled at her fine dress so roughly he tore the ruffle. He ripped her panties off and raped her with what seemed like all the force he could muster up. His forceful entrance tore her vagina wall. It felt as if he ripped the delicate layer of skin inside her to pieces. Chasah remembers being afraid and hurt. She remembers the tears. She remembers his threats and how he said she better act like she liked it. She remembers that horrific night very well.

She could still hear his voice say, *"Make me believe you, or I'll cut your throat."*

He also demanded that she rotate her hips, or the knife would make its way to her chest. She did as she was told. She did everything he commanded. She held her breath and touched her lips with his. She was careful not to let her tongue touch his tongue or his lips. She held it back hoping he wouldn't notice or care. She wanted to scream as she moved her hips in a circular motion. The scream was stuck in her chest. She couldn't pull it up for fear he'd make good on his threats.

Chasah stayed home for the rest of winter break. She didn't leave the house for any reason, except school for months after. Her uncle walked her to the bus stop every morning and he met her for the walk home in the afternoon. He stood there strongly each day when she got off that bus. Chasah loved her uncle, he acted like the father she didn't have. She was afraid to go out alone and he knew it. Chasah missed Jake, but those feelings were overshadowed by her fear of going out alone. She checked his Twitter Page. No activity. Snapchat. No activity. Instagram. No activity.

Chasah did not see Jake at school after winter break. She asked a few people if they'd seen him, they said no. Chasah could not understand what happened. She sent him a text. *"Message undeliverable."* She was so lonely and afraid, still. She felt so distraught from the attack. This made her open and vulnerable. She tried to go to his Facebook page and leave another message, but his page had disappeared.

Chasah saw the new transfer student, Gideon, in the cafeteria. They made eye contact. His stare was immediately intense, but it didn't unnerve her. He sat at the table in front of her with a friend. She could hardly focus on eating her lunch for watching him. As soon as their eyes met, she felt anger, instead of worry, for Jake. *Where was he and how could he disappear without one word?* She missed him. The last time she called his cell, she got a recording saying the number was disconnected. She used her break to read ahead for her next class. Gideon walked over to where she was and sat next to her. She was intrigued by the way he greeted her.

"Shalom Lil Princess."

"What does that mean? Does that mean the same as A salaam alaikum?"

"My name is Gideon."

Gideon began to explain his greeting and his name. She liked the way he explained things. He was gentle. He wasn't Jake, but his voice comforted her. Chasah admired his boldness.

27

Being shy and a bit of an introvert, it was easy to talk back to him. All she could do was answer his questions. She liked his name. Gideon. It was typical for her to shudder away and clamor up when approached by new people. She noticed she didn't stutter with Gideon though. He made her smile when he asked, *"Do you think you and I have a chance together?"*

She didn't know how to respond to his question since there was no break-up with Jake. In each moment, she listened and responded. She evaluated her reactions and attempted to come up with some sort of a catchy and hip phrase to say but couldn't and it didn't seem to matter to Gideon. She felt her face smiling and she felt the memory of Jake slowly slip to the back of her mind. She wanted to respond with something catchy or hip something memorable that he would think about later. She was a little excited, but uncertain.

She was nervous but felt a little bit of the loneliness leave her. She needed comfort and Gideon would do just fine. He seemed different from the other men her age around her. She felt like he could protect her. She felt safe, she never felt this safe with Jake. Gideon reminded her of how kind-hearted her Uncle Ray used to be. It was like she was being covered by a tented sanctuary; she didn't feel like a possession.

She felt freedom and safety when Gideon asked,
"Can I walk with you to your next class?"

2

At the End of the Day

Kayla loved to hear her daughter Keila and her oldest son Kaleb sing old school music. Kayla's love for R&B, especially blues, was passed on to her children. However, Keila still seemed to view the world and rhythm to the sounds of hip hop and rap music. Kayla hated it, but she tolerated it in the house for the sake of her daughter Keila and the other children feeling comfortable at home. She did not want them to feel like they had to steal away to their friend's homes, where parents were more lenient. Kayla did not mind Keila sitting in the living room playing her CD's. She knew Keila would be careful.

Kayla purchased a calendar a few years ago. Each month had an image of a different praise dancer. The calendar was adorned with images of praise dancers giving glory, honor and praise to the Heavenly Father through the ministry of dance and music. At the end of that year, she cut out the images, framed them, and hung the 12 lovely images throughout her apartment. They reminded her to keep her head in the right place.

A thought came to her mind as she looked at the praise dancers on her wall.

"I don't think I have ever felt this good in my life," she spoke loudly.

As she laid her clothes out for the next day, she thought about the difficulties she had trying to earn a college degree and raising her children alone. Then, according to her bitter aunt, she had the audacity to enroll in classes for business and marketing. She wanted to use her passion for crafting to open her own business. She thought it would be smart to study business and marketing first to help ensure her business' success.

It takes most people four years to finish a simple BA. It took Kayla eight years to finish because of her responsibilities of caring for her children. In each moment, she relished the time she spent with her children. Though she had the academic skills, she wanted to properly take care of her babies, because they meant a lot to her. She was not going to let life make her bitter.

It takes time to nurture and rear children properly. Kayla was proud of herself. She finally did it; they were all almost out of high school and adults! She wanted to encourage other single mothers to have enough courage, patience and pride within themselves and to pass it to their daughters and sons. Kayla didn't think about being alone as much as she used to. She spent her time just trying to get through each day. She was free to love, yet nobody was in her life who wanted to love her. She was fine with that. She learned that one does not have to be lonely when they are alone. In each moment, she contemplated the joys of freedom; she knew it was going to be another lovely day the Lord made, and she was getting better at rejoicing when faced with another day.

Growing up in Chicago and battling the harsh winters, Kayla loved the lakefront beaches, the parks, and the zoo. She loved spending her time listening to the percussionists engage in their regular jam sessions at the 63rd Street beach. She was afraid to get out there herself with her Shakore', so she used her fingers to tap out the beats on her steering wheel. Kayla also liked to read while she sat there or watch the families have such a great time barbecuing and picnicking outside the beach area. There was always something free to do on the lakefront in Chicago, especially in the summer. In the winter, there was always something to do throughout the city.

Kayla liked the line dance classes in Dolton on Thursday nights. She still loved to dance.

Being the place where stepping was created, Kayla could always find a steppers class to attend that didn't cost too much. This way, she was entertained and got in a good workout at the same time. Dancing kept her looking good. The museums were fantastic, and they still had one free day each week for visitors like Kayla. Even though gang violence was taking over some areas of the city, Chicago was a marvelous place and she loved living there. She didn't mind doing anything alone anymore. Besides it was much better than being someone's temp or side piece. Besides, Kayla was waiting to be found by her Boaz.

It was finally getting warm and the sun shone longer, giving her more daylight to walk on the lake. Kayla rushed out of the house to pick up the boys from school and take them to baseball practice. She'd arranged for her sister to pick up Keila and take her to the *Daughters of Sarah* class at the Knesset. She felt accomplished to have been able to be consistent with keeping herself and the children active in the Knesset for so long. She was hoping one of the brothers would try and date her, but she guessed they were afraid of a sister with three children.

She had time to stop at the same Walgreens where she always stopped. She wanted to pick up some Emergen-C packets before the boys finished. She parked her car at the back of the parking lot as she always did to ensure she increased the number of steps she took every day. It was easy to reach her goal of 10,000 steps every day and it was not uncommon for her Apple watch to report 15,000 steps when she made time to take those walks on the lake.

As Kayla got out of the car, put her earphones in her ear and walked across the parking lot, she was almost run into by a dark colored van. She held her phone case tightly in her hand, as it was important. It held her whole life. Her credit card was in it, work ID, driver's license, insurance card and all the stuff she needed, instead of a large cumbersome purse. The same homeless gentlemen she saw last time as she entered the store stood there again asking people to use the ATM inside.

"Can you go to the ATM and get some money out, and help me?"

Whatever happened to people asking for a lil change? The last time she gave him $1. That's all she had. She didn't usually have cash or coins on hand. He asked her for a dollar.

"I don't have one," Kayla snapped. She wasn't even to the door yet.

"How about when you come out!"

Kayla kept walking. She walked deliberately down the aisle to get to where she knew she'd find the Emergen-C packs. The store didn't seem so crowded on the way in, and she got through the check out pretty quickly. *"Early evening is a good time to go to Walgreens,"* she thought as she swiped her card to check out. Her main thoughts though were to get to the park before baseball practice ended. She didn't like them waiting outside for her. She wanted to be there as they came out of the door. She wanted her boys to be safe and she feared children being alone unsupervised in the park, especially so close to sundown. She had to then get to the Knesset to pick up Keila before her *Daughters of Sarah* class ended. *"Darn!"*, remembering she wanted to get that quick walk on the lake in also. That might not happen this evening.

When Kayla walked out of the store the homeless man said, *"Can I get a dollar now?"*

Kayla was suddenly pissed. She quickly and quietly responded, *"For one, they don't give dollars."* She felt insulted. *"Didn't you just get a check on the first?"*

"That was three days ago," eased out of his mouth so easily.

"HELL NO!" thought Kayla. Instead, she retorted, *"You didn't give ME none of that!"*

With gall, the beggar said, *"You didn't ask."*

Kayla was too through and she sped up her walk to the car across the parking lot. She noticed her right shoestring was loose but would wait to tie it when she got her boys in the car. One stop was enough. She noticed the same dark van approaching ahead of her and to her right, so she walked closer to the parked cars on her left. One thing she didn't want to happen was to get ran over by some no driving, indecisive driver. The van slowed down and seemed come too close as it seemed to pass her. Kayla slowed down to let the van pass, her aim was to pick up her babies on time.

The parking lot was just about empty. The van came to an abrupt stop. The side door was snatched open and a white man with dark hair and a black hoodie jumped out of the van, grabbed her in an almost bear hug, and threw her in the van, before jumping in himself and slamming it shut. Kayla screamed in astonishment as she was snatched. She dropped her bag, keys and phone case. The police arrived after being called by an older woman sitting in her car. She'd seen everything.

"It happened so fast!" she screamed.

The police found her right shoe where Kayla was accosted in plain view of the security camera.

3

Under a Dark Shadow

The first time Aliyah heard him, she stood in the bathroom listening through their shared wall for ten minutes and debated over what would happen if she called the landlord to report the disturbance. Living in this large building was very different from living in the duplex over a senior citizen couple, Abah Hosea and Emah Adeevah, and their two cats in the South Suburbs. She really missed the place. She felt safe there. They treated her like a daughter and called her baht. She was sad Abah Hosea passed away so suddenly. She was perplexed when their son came from LA to put his own mother in a nursing home and sell her home out from under her.

Aliyah tried to tell Robert she would care for his mother, but he wasn't having it. He obviously didn't want to take care of his own mother, yet he wouldn't allow her to do it, and she wanted to. Aliyah thought of Emah Adeevah as the grandmother she never had. She loved the attention Emah gave her daughter Naomi. Aliyah thought it would be a better idea for Robert to take his mother back to California with him. He wouldn't think of that either.

As Aliyah listened to the voice coming from the other side of the bathroom wall, she felt a tingle in her legs. After a few minutes, she wasn't disturbed any longer but intrigued. He was always so loud, but he had a really good voice. Unlike hers, it was made for singing. During the five weeks she'd lived in the building, she never heard a female voice coming from behind the other side of the wall.

"Is he married? Or does he have a lady friend? He sounds like he could be a little older, not much, but maybe a little? What does he do for a living? Is he a singer for real? If he is, then why doesn't he sing any original songs? So, he must not be a real singer? Then what does he do? Why don't I ever see?"

Aliyah was not disturbed anymore. Instead she had questions. She'd decided the next time she heard his key in the door next to hers, then she'd make up a reason to go out into the hallway.

"What does he look like?" she thought out loud.

She left the bathroom because she felt like an intruder listening to her next-door neighbor in his bathroom.

"OOO, this ain't right," she murmured. Before turning to leave though she decided to knock on the wall.

"Sh, sh, sh", she uttered loudly as she knocked.

She was startled by the sudden silence. Then he began to sing again. This time though, she could tell he tried to lower his voice.

"Well at least he is thoughtful," she said to herself as she left the bathroom to go into her bedroom.

Teaching at South Suburban Community College Early College was Aliyah Dauid's first assignment. She chose her outfit carefully. It was a pink and gray business suit she got from Ashley Stuarts' clearance rack. She wanted to get her feet securely in the door and get past the 90-day probationary period before breaking out in full garb.

As she looked at herself in the mirror, she asked herself, *"Who the hell are you?"*

Aliyah knew she needed to be more conscious of what she ate, and she needed to work out. She hated her size. She didn't remember when she gained the extra pounds, but she had a difficult time finding an outfit that fit and would give her the professional look she sought. She wanted to make a good first impression on her colleagues as well as her students. She was eager and very nervous about this position.

Initially, Aliyah wanted to teach eighth grade at a middle school. She wasn't sure if she could handle the maturity of today's high school students. However, after being overlooked for the perfect position twice, she felt she better take this job. It would give her the experience she needed to re-apply for the position she really wanted. She spent the entire evening before preparing for her debut as an English teacher. She wanted to make sure she got her bluff in right away with these students.

SSC Early College was known to be a little rough. She reviewed several issues of The T.R.U.S.T. Restorative Classroom Management manual taking note of common occurrences she might face tomorrow. If she could survive at an alternative high school for at-risk youth, she could survive anywhere. She carefully chose a reading assignment that might be of interest to the students. It was a short story about a family struggling to make it and overcoming many trials and tribulations. She wanted to encourage her students to have courage, patience, and pride within themselves. Aliyah decided to have her students read the story she chose and write about how much strength and pride the family in the story needed to make it through their day.

She let her daughter Naomi read the story for approval. She was ten years old going on forty. Naomi was very mature for her age, because she was an avid reader. She was glad her daughter was not born a boy. She feared a boy would genetically hold Benjamin's darkness. She felt like she could better influence a daughter to be good inside by being her example.

Naomi missed her Abah. Before they left, Aliyah made sure she wrote Benjamin a long letter explaining he could see Naomi anytime he wanted. She told him she preferred to drop Naomi off at Softah's house whenever they wanted to see her. He was to call her sister Linda to make visiting arrangements. Aliyah thought it through thoroughly. She also went to his Emah's house and let her know the plan too. She never told Softah where she lived, so Softah would not have to lie to her son.

Aliyah loved Benjamin's Emah; she was always kind to her. How could Aliyah make Emah understand, Benjamin made her fear for her life? Before she left, Aliyah explained to his mom her plan and why she felt she had to go.

Emah smiled at her and said, *"I know sweetheart, I was married to Benjamin's daddy, remember."* Then she gave Aliyah a long tight squeeze. *"You are a brave young woman, be happy. Just don't forget your God."*

Softah had been asking for Naomi one weekend a month for the past six months when she got her social security check. Naomi enjoyed being at Softah's house baking and working in her garden. Softah loved for Naomi to read to her at night. Benjamin never came to see Naomi while she was at Softa's house, and he never left a message for a special visit either.

When Benjamin wanted to support Naomi financially, he could deposit money into an account with Naomi's name on it at the Chase Bank right down the street from him or leave it with Softah. Aliyah tried to make it easy, but she was not going to beg; or take him to court for child support. She was going to let that be between him and Yah. In the meantime, she got on her knees everyday asking Yah to provide for her baby since her daddy would not.

It was common to find both Aliyah and Naomi curled up on the chaise lounge together in their new place reading. They read silently as well as out loud to each other. Like Aliyah, Naomi has always been academic levels above the rest of her class. There was a bookshelf in every room, including the bathroom and kitchen. Aliyah was a mother who spent much time with her little girl. She became interested in teaching as she volunteered at Naomi's school and helped her with her homework. Just before Naomi's sixth birthday, Aliyah organized a play group, which met once per week at her apartment.

Aliyah felt safe living in the high rise in Hyde Park, because they had tight security, and no one could get on the elevator unless they were expected. The security guard always checked. She never discussed any of this with Naomi; she was very careful not to talk badly to her daughter about her dad. She was trying to do the right thing. She simply wanted peace and love, of course.

Aliyah loved to hear Naomi sing old school music. It was a kind of family legacy. The music of the late sixties 60's to mid-70's, where lyrics were less important than rhythm and actual musical instruments. Aliyah's father was a master drummer and he caused her to appreciate good music. Now, Aliyah wanted her daughter Naomi to learn to appreciate pure music just like her father taught her to love it.

"Emah, can I get an IPOD when you get your first paycheck?", asked Naomi.

"Let's talk about it after the third or fourth paycheck," Aliyah said. *"The rent is paid for only one more month, I ain't buying no extra stuff for a while,"* she said to herself.

Aliyah loved art and decor that depicted her heritage. Her house was filled with pictures of mothers and their children, praise dancers who seemed to be having a good time, as well as men working and taking care of business. She purchased a piece from an auction that was simply a giant West African baobab tree standing strong and firm near a body of water, as she knew her people to be. There was a mountain and waterfall behind it. The tree reminded her of the nobility and the strength of those first "migrants" stolen from the shores of their homeland and shipped to a land of criminal strangers. This piece gave Aliyah a feeling of peace and serenity. She hung it on the wall at the foot of her bed.

As she laid her clothes out on the sofa, she thought about the difficulties she had trying to finish high school and raise a child alone. Then, she found the courage to enroll in college. Her own mother told her she needed to go get a job. It takes most people four years to finish college. It took Aliyah six. She wanted a different life, a better one, a life with more quality. That takes time. She was proud of herself. She finally did it! She was much better than Popeye's Chicken.

"Oooo, that's my song!" She stopped her reflective moment to dance. *"Ooh-ooh-oh-ooh-oh-ooh-Ooh-ooh-oh-ooh-Ooh, yeah, baby. Whoa-whoa-oh-oh-Mmm…"*

Aliyah allowed her body to get wrapped up in the music. In each moment, she listened, she snapped her fingers and let her arms and feet be moved by the rhythm behind the words. *"It's so nice to have a man around to lend a helping hand, you can bet. Yeah!"* mumbled Aliyah, as she danced to the Temptations.

This song was not necessarily an old skool jam, but shoot, Aliyah thought. *"Cause I believe a woman should be treated with the utmost respect, mmm-hmmm…"* she danced and sang along.

"Whoa whoa, oh oh, mmm…, I need a man to touch me," she added.

Aliyah wasn't sure whether she missed Benjamin because she yearned to be touched or

45

because she really desired his company. She hadn't let herself think about him in a while and she wouldn't now either. He didn't deserve her thoughts.

"Now I like openin' doors, Pickin' up Yeah, her hanky Yeah off the floor. Treat her like a lady..." she sang along.

The song made her feel like she missed out on being treated well. She was not a feminist, and women's lib was not her thing, so the words to the song caused her to want a man to open doors for her and block the traffic keeping her safe as she crossed the street. It made her long for the compliments from a man such as the lyrics described. As she listened to the tempting Temptations sing to her, she thought about the couple who lived next door. He treated his wife this way. Aliyah never experienced that type of treatment, yet she longed for it. She was happy for her neighbors.

"Who's gonna touch me?", Aliyah lamented softly to herself. She didn't want Naomi to hear her.

The music gave her something to look forward to. It made her feel the possibilities and the hope of love. She did not want to forget that. The music gave her hope. She closed her eyes, bobbed her head, and let the music permeate her.

"Man, that's my song, one day someone is going to love me," she muttered again as a tear made its way down her cheek. She sat down in her favorite chair and just snapped her fingers and bobbed her head and moaned, *"Man, sometimes it hurts."* She said too loudly.

"What did you say Emah?" shouted Naomi from her room.

"Nothin lil girl, just singing my song. You are playing Emah some good music this evening." Aliyah shouted back to her. She was a Temptations buff.

It was Benjamin's touch that held her hostage. She needed to stop toying with herself before she picked up the phone to call him to tell him where they'd moved. She missed being touched. Instead, she remembered the sickened pain she felt in the pit of her stomach the last time she saw him as he stood outside her car peering at her through his sunglasses as he told her that she was never in his corner, because she wouldn't skip her class to go with him to pick up his new business cards before the print shop closed.

"You want to wear the pants in this relationship. You probably gonna meet some other nigga."

47

Benjamin was a skilled teacher. In fact, that is what drew Aliyah to Benjamin in the first place. He knew his way around the Book. She was excited for him and proud he was teaching Bible class that night, she hoped it would change him. She hadn't been to Thursday night Bible class since the semester started. She didn't think it was an occasion to miss an important psychology class. He didn't like her choice.

"Why you can't believe I love you and I'm not trying to be with nobody else. I want to make this work with you," she begged. *"I'm glad you are teaching tonight and I believe you will do well, but I can't miss class tonight. I will go back after this semester is over,"* she promised.

She loved encouraging him, but he couldn't find it in his heart to share in her moments as well. He took submission too far. He accused her of not knowing how to submit, but he didn't know how to cause her to want to submit.

Suddenly, Aliyah remembered that Benjamin was the reason she was ostracized. He told one brother at Bible class she slept with some brother at the university and the lie spread like wildfire. At Sabbath fellowship, the brothers wouldn't allow their wives to talk to her. She looked Amirah in her face and greeted her with a warm happy *"Shalom"*, but Amirah gave her a stony face and did not return her greeting. When she took time and care to clean, fold, and deliver books, lightly used toys, and baby clothes to

Sister Eve, her husband, brother Jeremiah, returned them to Aliyah.

"My wife can't accept these from you," he stabbed.

Aliyah knew why these things were happening to her and she refused to defend herself to these people, these friends, who were supposed to be her family. The feast committee would not even accept her food she tried to contribute to the last feast. This was Benjamin's family; they were not hers. They proved that when they turned on her because of his lies. The effects of this horrible secret really devastated her when it spilled over into another part of their lives. Benjamin gas-lighted her whenever he did not want to take responsibility for his actions. He tried to make her think it was her fault; as if she did something to cause him to do it. He was skillful in this deceit and she was becoming as good at it as he was. Each time he promised this was the last time.

When Aliyah and Benjamin were alone one night, she asked him why he kept reneging on his promise to stop. Aliyah's heart dropped to her feet as she felt a tinge of blood fall to her cheek from the corner of her mouth. As she continued to feel the throbbing of his fists on her injured, now bruised face and on her battered chest as he straddled her, she could not twist her torso enough to get away from his fist in her stomach. She remembered all the times

Benjamin used his tongue to abuse her and fists to assault her over and over again. This time because she merely questioned him.

"A submissive wife will never question her head," he shouted. *"Why do you always make me punish you? If I don't punish you, The Most High will, and you won't like it. Believe me. It will not feel good. He will have your eternal soul."*

"I'm sorry Lord, please forgive me for questioning you," Aliyah shrieked loudly as she tried to twist her body from Benjamin's grips.

"Look at you, you are still not submissive, you refuse to take your punishment. Who is Lord of this house? Who is head? Who wears the pants?"

When Aliyah woke up, she was lying on the couch and Benjamin was kneeled over her telling her to wake up. Naomi was standing in the doorway watching and listening. *What were they teaching her? What example was she setting for her daughter?*

"You need to be more submissive and obey your lord. If you don't, I will get another wife to show you how it is done. No other brother in the fellowship has this problem with their wives. You are an embarrassment and I will take great pleasure in breaking your Jezebel spirit. You

cannot question me; I am your teacher and I am your lord!", he cried with literal tears.

In the 10 years they were together, Benjamin accused Aliyah of trying to wear the pants in the family and jeopardizing his lordship and reign many times, but it was never this ruthless. This was not just the usual back hand or smack in the face. On a few occasions, her punishment was a whooping with his leather belt as if she were a mischievous child. This battering was finally the catalyst for her to leave him. Emotional abuse has scars the world cannot see, but when coupled with physical abuse, it is a devastating and incapacitating knock-out punch combination. *How can a woman love a man who beats her?*

Finally, after years of living in terror, Aliyah mustered up enough strength and courage to remove herself and her child from the grips of the mean man and his lack of confidence. She learned a man who lacks confidence in himself and in God is a dangerous man, whom no woman can change. She was labeled a whore, a sinful woman, a liar, and an unruly female who wanted to lead her husband instead of allowing him to lead her. The whole "family" feared her.

Aliyah feared these same people who feared her, because she was afraid of how judgmental and unforgiving, she learned they could be. They didn't care to realize a good woman doesn't leave a good man without good cause. Benjamin was the kind of man who loved intensely, but more times than not, he was extremely incompetent as a benevolent husband.

Aliyah feared she'd be alone for the rest of her life. In each moment, she lived without the fellowship of the so-called "sisters and brothers" who abandoned her, she thought about living this life of fear and realized she was not afraid of death at all. Her greatest fear was being alone. Aliyah felt stupid for even thinking of picking up the phone. She didn't have to fight making that call anymore. She remembered why she walked away, and she felt sick and tired of being accused of not being in his corner when it was him who was not in her corner.

Aliyah was afraid of Benjamin's lies he spread through the "family" to cover his tracks, because he believed, with all his being, she was the cause. She feared things would get worse as his insecurities grew. The more she tried making their lives better, the worse he got.

"Stop it, don't be stupid. You know how it will end. Let him go. He doesn't need to know where we are", she reminded herself. Aliyah thanked Yah for the escape. As soon as she was settled in her new place and her new job, she would find someplace else to fellowship on the Sabbath. She missed fellowship, but she'd never stop living the lifestyle and she never stopped teaching it to her daughter and being her example.

"Naomi, it's almost time for bed. You can stop being the DJ now. Do you have your clothes and book bag ready for tomorrow? We don't want to get up with too many things to do in the morning.

I cannot be late for my first day," she shouted
redirecting her own thoughts more than
instructing the little DJ in the other room.

She was not going to let her thoughts take her
back there, and she was not going to be
distracted from making her first assignment a
good experience for her students. *"Get a grip
girl, keep the darkness at bay."*

As Aliyah put her baby girl to bed and
listened to her nightly ritual of saying ten things
for which her daughter was thankful, thoughts of
the man who sang through her bathroom wall
went in and out of her head until the next song
on the playlist took over her thoughts
completely. Aliyah began to be angry with
herself for wanting to make that call. She was
simply lonely and wanted to be touched.

"I need the comfort of a man," sang Stephanie
Mills to Aliyah's lonely heart as she closed her
eyes and imagined a man who was kind, loving,
yet strong and protective. She dreamed of a man
who was filled with The Fruit of the Spirit. She
wanted him almost desperately. *"I need to
change to gospel music to get my mind in a
different place,"* as she switched to a different
playlist. *"How about No Woman No Cry by Bob
Marley,"* she said aloud. *"This may change my
mood a bit.*

4

A Time to Love

Reuben didn't like being alone anymore. He couldn't remember when he wasn't alone. Though he worked two jobs and had people around him most of the time, his heart was in teaching. Reuben reflected on his work at the Los Angeles Community College, where he taught Criminal Justice. He thought about Richard, a young man in his Wednesday morning class.

Reuben had taught only a few young men like Richard in his four years as a college professor. He could see loneliness in the young man's eyes and suspected he was at his wit's end. Being a friend to loneliness, he knew it well. He invited Richard to join the spoken word group he chaperoned. He was playing psychologist and figured Richard would connect to the group, because of the brotherhood aura he created in the group. Reuben enjoyed mentoring young men and encouraging them to live in the hood, but not be of it.

He chose the proverbial black slacks to wear today. This time, he decided to go with a peach shirt and mildly colorful tie. His dress was usually very conservative. When Reuben left home that morning, he had a feeling it would be a special day.

Today he dressed in preparation for the blessing he knew he'd attract.   After tying the tie snugly around his neck, he spotted the tweed jacket that went with his black pants. It was early spring, and mornings could be a bit nippy in the east wing of the college. Reuben wasn't new to the department chair position. His office was always chilly, and he wouldn't miss feeling that chill at all.

He was leaving in less than a week and Reuben felt melancholy about his West Coast days coming to an end. While preparing his usual breakfast of coffee, English muffins, and fresh melon salad, Reuben couldn't help but remember the reasons he was going back home to Chicago.

He'd be near his family, whom he missed, and he'd planned to make a real impact on the lives of young men in Chicago, who needed what he had to offer. Before going to his last meeting for department chairpersons, Reuben stopped by the registrar's office to submit his final grades. This was his last semester as Professor Reuben Dauid. He was moving to the Chicago Suburb of Homewood to start a new job as the principal of an alternative high school. He was anxious to be of service and sure the work would fulfil him. Plus, he'd be closer to his ailing father so he could help.

———————————————

As Reuben entered the building of South Suburban Early College to start his new job his eyeballs caught sight of a fine sister in a pink and gray business suit, sauntering up the hallway towards him. He could sense she wasn't aware of the sensuality in her walk, she just walked. Her walk wasn't sexy, it was regal. She walked like a queen.

Reuben could sense her eagerness to teach. As he watched her walk into the office, he wondered if she would bring his blessing that day. *"She seemed to have chosen the outfit for her first day with care",* Reuben thought. Her attire was stylish and had a flare of elegance, yet it was businesslike and professional. He spotted the pink that faintly appeared between the wool woven tightly together. The straight skirt accented her full figure. Yet the black wool made her stout curves appear slim.

Reuben loved a woman with a little meat on her bones. When he decided to choose a woman, he wanted one he could hold on to. He wanted one he could feel. He wanted to find out who this beautiful woman was. He imagined her warm smile seeming to invite him into her life. He wondered if she was already married or dating. Her ring finger was empty with no shadow. He wondered if she was soon to occupy at least some of his lonely time.

Reuben intentionally sped up his walk to catch up to her, so they'd get to the main office at the same time. He walked ahead to ensure he got to the office first. In each moment, he waited for her as he opened the door, held it in a gentlemanly manner so she could enter first, and greeted her with a kind and exhilarating smile, being careful not to be flirtatious as she walked in.

The smile he received in return was not standoffish, she was warm. Reuben could tell she held back deliberately, as she retained her regal air. In the back of his mind he felt he needed to be a better him, the expectation made his heart really flutter. His aim was to make this a special day as he contemplated the best way to make her smile. He knew it was time. He wanted to cause her to smile every day for the remainder of her life. In each moment, he thought about it, he remembered he was the new principal, he was the boss. *"I'm going to need a new job,"* he began to plan.

5

Taste of Love

Yohanathan's Emah and Abah met in college, on the campus of Tuskegee University in the itty bitty city of Tuskegee, Alabama. His father was from the Southside of Chicago, and his mother was a native of Alabama ready to leave the first chance she got. She never understood why her family did not leave the south during The Great Migration. Her uncles left with the second wave in 1940. When her father came back from World War II, he decided to remain on the family land outside of Birmingham, Alabama and make the land work for him. Her father regretted his decision later, but was committed to the idea, so he stayed. Both her parents came from Black middle-class families with two parents in the home. In 1961, Yohanathan's mother and father entered the Tuskegee Institute graduating class together unbeknownst to one another until they met at Homecoming that year, when their love story began.

After they both graduated in 1961, they got married in 1962. Then, the newlyweds settled in Chicago, a few blocks from his mother's uncle and his family. The young couple started a real estate business. Their first purchase was a building on 47th in Bronzeville. The building had three small store fronts and four apartments above them. His father chose one store for his office and his mom opened a small Chicken and Waffles restaurant in another. She was a good cook and businesswoman. Both the businesses flourished. Yohanathan's parents rented the third storefront to a couple with whom they graduated, both Black doctors who serviced the segregated Southside community. They lived in one of the apartments and rented the others. It was a time when there were thriving businesses in the Black Chicago area and Yohanathan's parents were among them.

In 1968, after the death of Dr. Martin Luther King Jr., his parents attended a meeting of the Original Hebrew Israelite Nation on the city's South Side in search of self-identity and self-awareness. During those times, self was indicative to the Black community, rather than an individual person, very unlike today where the opposite exists. It was a time of Black unrest and White upheaval in the country. During Dr. King's fight against segregation in Chicago in 1966, Yohanathan's father said the mobs in Chicago were more hateful than the ones he'd experienced in Alabama and Mississippi. He described Chicago as a hateful and closed society. He set about helping the Blacks in Chicago open it up and Yohanathan's parents joined in the fight.

His parents joined the Chicago Freedom Movement when Yohanathan was just a boy. He remembered their fight against everything which helped to keep Chicago segregated: slumlords, realtors and Mayor Richard J. Daley's Democratic machine. It was a time when a revolution in black consciousness and an awakening was about to sweep the country. They found answers among the teachings of the Torah, as interpreted for them by two black "rabbis," Robert Divine and his assistant, Yehoshuah Sample. The teachers explained that the Black Hebrews were the direct descendants of the patriarchs, Abraham, Isaac and Jacob and the 10 lost tribes, who had been exiled from Israel for their sins and condemned to wander throughout Africa until they were kidnapped and sold into slavery in the Americas.

The day Dr. King was murdered, the school let the children out early. Yohanathan didn't know why until he got home. The teachers and principals cried as they dismissed the children. The walk home was quiet and dismal. The children knew something was wrong but did not know what until they reached their homes where parents were gathered around the television watching the news and getting angrier by the minute. Yohanathan witnessed rioting in the streets of Chicago, in his own neighborhood.

The assassination of Dr. King incited Black people to burn down businesses in their own communities. He saw the National Guard at the end of one corner and rioting looters at the other end. He witnessed a young White UPS driver ripped from his truck and beaten unmercifully by three young Black men. He saw looters carrying merchandise they hadn't purchased from the Woolworth's on the corner. He saw a Black barber standing outside his shop pleading with the rioters not to burn down his barber shop.

The year before, many families left the U.S. with Black Hebrew leader Ben Ami. After the riots, more families left, including Yohanathan's best friend James. Yohanathan's parents were tempted to leave the country as well. They chose to remain in Chicago instead. They made the decision to stay because in order to join the group they were required to sell their possessions, as Jesus directed the rich man, and turn the money over to the leaders of the group who would make travel arrangements and send a message regarding when it was time to leave. The money was also to be used for the sake of the group who mingled black history with the reading of the Old Testament.

The group adopted the ideas of Marcus Garvey, who led the Back-to-Africa movement in the 1920's. On an ultimate migration to the homeland of Israel, the leaders decided to direct people to settle in Liberia to purify the people first. Many never made it to Israel and those who did suffered hardship and came close to starvation first. The people who were able to return to Chicago, told stories of woe and adversity.

Yohanathan heard his parents say years later, after hearing about the hardships and sufferings of some people who left from personal friends who returned, that this was one of the best decisions they could have made for their family. The family never became members of a camp again, but they taught Yohanathan and his siblings how to live a lifestyle of righteousness. They closed their businesses every Saturday to observe the Sabbath and celebrated Holy Days. There were always a few families who joined them in the large backyard of their building for these celebrations.

Yohanathan remembers they never ate pork or shellfish again after they joined the Black Hebrew group. His mother even stopped serving it in her restaurant. Instead she served lamb chops, salmon, and red snapper. Yohanathan's favorite. They were committed to the new lifestyle and they taught their children to be committed to it as well. Yohanathan remembered very little of his pre-Black Hebrew life.

It was on the 4th day of The Feast of Tabernacles when Yohanathan looked up and watched his heart walk through the door of the restaurant. She was dressed in a midriff peach dress. The waist fit just tight enough to see she was a brick house and the bottom was wide enough for the air from the closing door to swish it lightly as if it were leaves on a tree. She wore it with a white lace wrap around her shoulders and a peach head wrap that looked as if it were wrapped for the queen of Ethiopia. He knew she would be his wife.

He graduated college the year prior and was to take over his father's real-estate business within a year upon his retirement. He had already made a few deals on his own so, his father knew the business would be in good hands. As Yohanathan watched her walk into the restaurant, he began to plan to love her and treat her with benevolence.

Six months later, Yohanathan tasted Ranya's mind and realized he had been starving for a gorgeous Israelite sister who could discuss The Word of God with intellect. They'd gotten to know each other well. They talked about everything. One day, while they talked about the reasons why Ruth and Boaz attracted each other's attention, he wanted nothing more than to sit with her under the stout swietenia humilis tree in the backyard of his winter home nestled in the beautiful mountains of Yalbac Hills in the Cayo district of Belize. Yohanathan loved his little haven in Central America. It was amazing that a young man of thirty-eight was able to earn enough money in real estate to purchase land in another country.

The striking swietenia humilis tree, which sprouts genuine mahogany wood, reminded him of the Baobab tree he saw sitting near the shores of the Bight of Benin in West Africa when he took his last trip.   The tree was taller than a skyscraper in the city where he was born and at least as wide as half a football field. Yohanathan was a hopeless romantic, like his father and his grandfather. He was the third Yohanathan and he promised himself he'd teach his own sons to romance their wives as well. The tree in the backyard of his winter home was a symbol of his love for Ranya, which means song of God.

Yohanathan's mother taught him to respect women. His father taught him to never be ashamed to show kindness to his woman. Even when his parents argued, they were careful not to use hurtful words that they would later regret. There is no way to take those hurtful words back once they come out of your mouth. They practiced the skill of not letting the sun go down on wrath. He remembered them staying up many nights until they worked out their issues. And yet, you really didn't even know they were in the midst of an argument, because when their anger was heightened, they did not speak to one another above a whisper. Yohanathan learned they did this intentionally. It was one of the agreements of their marriage.

Yohanathan's father taught him to listen to his wife and to respect her opinion. He smiled each time he remembered his mother telling his father, when she thought he was making a mistake, *"You are not Ananias and I will not be your Sapphira."* His mother was like the sparklers' children play with on the fourth of July. Not a firecracker, which made a lot of noise with no splendor, but a sparkler, which brings both joy and splendor.

Yohanathan's father also taught him that marriage is a partnership, not a slave versus superior situation. He cleaned the kitchen after his wife cooked. When she was out late, whether working, visiting the sick, or at her women's group prayer meetings, he cooked dinner. He never treated his wife like she was a mere servant. While many men thought of their wives that way, Yohanathan never saw his father treat his mother as such. They were in that thing together and because he was a loving head of the household, their marriage lasted.

The formula he witnessed was that neither of them rarely thought about themselves. His father worked every day to make his wife smile and his mother worked every day to make his father smile. They submitted to one another. He never heard his mother complain about anything his father did, she talked to his father when she was not satisfied.

Alternately, he never heard his father complain to his buddies about his mother, he talked to her about his displeasure. They communicated openly, without fear of reprisal from the other. And they were a happy Black family, a light to the community.

In a time when Black men failed to provide because the system was set up to cause them to fail, Yohanathan's father never stopped trying. When business deals went south and grant monies failed to come through, his father knew that his mother would not look down on him and disrespect him when he failed at anything, and he didn't always succeed. While at the same time, she respected him when he tried. When he made a mistake or fell, he apologized to both God and his wife, then he got up and kept trying.

After they became part of the Black Hebrew community, Yohanathan saw his father pray and sometimes he would have Yohanathan pray right there beside him. He told his son that a righteous man may fall as he tries to be perfect in his daily walk, but what makes him righteous is that he gets back up. It was the trying which helped to keep their family strong. In each moment, Yohanathan reflected on his father's example of a benevolent husband, he wanted the same for his own life. Malachi 2:14 says: *"The Most High is witness to he and the wife of his youth."* Yohanathan knew Ranya could help him be a better man.

Yohanathan was ready for marriage. His only desire was to have the words which flowed from Ranya's tongue to his ears, be words of a virtuous and praying woman. She had that covered well. As they sat under that tree, he could feel his iron sharpening her iron, and her iron sharpening his iron as a result. She elevated his thinking to a level where he felt as if it were that moment and the twinkling of the eye he longed for.

He wanted to make love to her mind before he made love to her body. He savored every moment as they waited until the day of their marriage. They were both committed to no intercourse before they got their marriage license and both their blood and spiritual families could bear witness to their joyous occasion. Everything about Ranya made Yohanathan want to sing a song of praise to The Most High.

Wedding plans were underway when Yohanathan received news that Ranya and her bridesmaid were in a serious car accident. He ran to his car and raced to the hospital to be by his betrothed's bedside. When he got to the 4th floor intensive care unit, he saw Ranya's father holding his wife tightly as she wept into his chest. Her father looked up and locked eyes with Yohanathan and he immediately knew.

6

My Father's Sins

I am Meerah, the firstborn daughter of Israel's first king. The day my Abah, my daddy, King Saul, met Samuel was a glorious day for my family. Me, Emah, and my sister Michal danced and pranced and sang glory to God for our new station. That is, until we heard God's prophecy; the king would do wicked in the nation. Emah was a praying woman, you see. So, she told us to remember to always pray in order to save ourselves from God's condemnation.

My heart fell to the floor, and from that day to this, I watched my Abah fall. Because I was young, he wouldn't listen to me and being a mere woman didn't help none either. So, shoot, I just sat back and watched the sparks fly. If only he had prayed every day and kept all the Lord's commandments. If only he had submitted to that which was good in God's sight. It hurt me greatly to see my daddy make those five grave mistakes and fall away from God's light. When the Lord's spirit left my father, and a bad one overtook him, we immediately witnessed a terrible darkness like night.

First, after that big battle with the Philistines, he panicked. Instead of praying, asking God to help him by making all rough edges smooth and all crooked paths straight; he took matters into his own hands and went contrary to the law of sacrifice by making an offering himself. He needed for Samuel, the priest, to make that burnt offering, because it was the law and he knew it. Samuel was on his way, but my daddy wouldn't wait.

Next, in his haste and impatience he did something real stupid. He told the people to eat the meat they brought back as spoils of war. There is order in how we do things, but he proclaimed they do it without properly taking out all the blood first. He had the gall to proclaim it would not be a sin against the Lord. They may as well have eaten it raw. He had no right to put himself in God's place and change the law. I didn't eat because I was too afraid of what I saw.

Then, I knew all hell was gone break loose when he made his third mistake. When he led that big battle and slew those Amalekites. He was told to utterly destroy all they had and leave nothing to spare. But by then, my daddy King Saul was beside himself. I was shocked when he didn't follow the

Lord's instruction. When I saw the Amalekite King and his best sheep, oxen, and lamb being paraded down the center of the street, I fell to my knees and asked The Lord's mercy, because I knew my Abah was headed for sure destruction. My Abah should'na been greedy and tried to save the best for himself was my deduction. He left just too much room for Satan's vile induction.

Now I know my story is getting kinda long, so I'm gone try to rap this up real quick When I heard my father make excuses for saving that king and lie about trying to keep the best of the spoils for himself, my stomach became sick. You can't lie to God and not expect a swift kick. I didn't know no more what made my daddy tick.

My father's sins tore our family apart. He was suddenly blinded by jealousy for David, my brother Jonathan's best friend. My poor sister Michal wasn't praying every day like me and Emah. She made it easy for our father to use her as a pawn. She was given to David as a prized bride, but in a short while vehemently ripped away. She was traded to another. Michal couldn't be with the man who really adored her, is what I heard my Emah say.

It was all too much for me to see, he began to walk so bitterly. All I wanted my Abah to do was repent and fall to his knees. But that evil spirit wouldn't let him do it. And Emah? Oh, she really had a fit. In each moment, I watched; but all I could do was pray, watch and sit.

My Abah's sins almost destroyed Israel's entire nation. So much for my family's great station. But when Israel first kept pushing God for a king, He did foretell of that king's condemnation; which was my father's fall from salvation. My Abah's sins don't call for no adoration. He was destined to fall from the start. My father's sins greatly pierced my heart. His rise and fall tore our family apart. But as for me, "Heal me, O LORD, and I shall be healed; save me, and I shall be saved: for thou is my praise," I continued to pray and do my part.

7

Victimized By My Own Brothers

I am falling apart. I feel like my best days are behind me. I can't shake it. I know I shamed my family and my Emah keeps telling me it's my fault. Why can't she see I'm hurt down deep in my bones? They made me the victim. They did not consider me at all. I am the sister of all brothers, who don't try to grow in the Fruit of the Spirit.

Though only six of my brothers are born of my mother, they all act the same. Leah, my mother, is not like my grandmother, Sarah. She never speaks up for me. She doesn't challenge my father or my brothers with the truth about their behavior. They get away with everything. She drives me crazy, thinking she must be quietly agreeable all the time, especially when wrongdoing runs rampant in our family. These boys are out of control. I am not going to disrespect her or anything but, these boys take things too far. When I have children, I am going to tell my sons when they are wrong.

Zilpah and Bilhah were a lot older than me, but they were my friends. We would meet in Bilhah's tent because Dodah Rachel gave her paint for her lips and hair ornaments for her hair. She shared them with me and Zilpah. I listened to them talk and make plans for the happy life with the husbands of their dreams. They anticipated a husband would find them and pay their bondage price, marry them and sweep them off to some exotic land where they would bare his children. This all changed when Emah and Dodah used them as pawns in their war as part of an ongoing rivalry for my Abah's attention. I couldn't sneak in Bilhah's tent anymore and Zilpah had her own lion's share of problems to deal with. My family took away my friends. Is there no happiness for me?

There weren't many women in our little community. All I wanted were friends. In my naivety, I devised a plan. I made a basket of great chunky coils from water hyacinth stems and rope. Then I baked a loaf of bread and I picked berries and added it to the basket. I made cassia and peppermint oils noted as unmistakable fragrances and calming aromatic properties and added them to the basket. I wanted to show myself friendly, so I went out to visit the women of Shechem, where we'd made camp and where my Abah purchased the land where he had pitched his tent.

That's when I laid my eyes on Shechem. He was the prince of the land, and he was fine! I know I should have stopped him, but it was like love at first sight. I let him take me. I did not protest when he humbled me. Our souls were drawn to one another.

He said he loved me, and I believed him. He spoke so tenderly, and I wasn't promised to anyone, so in my mind what might happen could only be good. I wanted to be promised to him. We made a big mistake, but he tried really hard to make it right. Shechem asked Abah for my hand, to be his wife. He wanted me! Dinah. I was going to be the wife of the prince of the land. I was going to get away from my brothers and all their issues. I was anxious and I was excited too, but I was also so very scared our secret would be uncovered.

My brothers' behavior is an exploitative stench in my nose. You see, they wouldn't listen. And now…my lovely Shechem, his father Hamor and all the men of their city lay dead at the gate by the hands of my hotheaded brothers, Simeon and Levi. I tried to tell them and my other nine brothers that Shechem knew me, because I gave consent. Yes, what Shechem and I did was a violation of my familial boundaries, but I loved him.

We had cultural differences we were willing to overcome. He was following the culture of his own people, seeking fair trade and being neighborly. Shechem wasn't looking for love, neither was I. Didn't my word matter?

Shechem sought to hide me in his house, even his father tried to manipulate us out of what we thought was our secret. My brothers claim they were concerned with me being treated like a whore.

They were really more concerned with
intermarriage among other nations than they were
about my virtue. Why couldn't my brothers hear my
voice? In their deceit, they thought they could
control who people love.

Upon hearing the news, Abah was silent at first;
then he tried to negotiate my marriage to Shechem.
He knew there was no need to protect me, Shechem
was tender, he was not violent. To Abah, he
appeared to be a man in love, not a man committing
a violent act of rape. He could see I had no feelings
of hostility and hatred toward Shechem, I didn't
hate him. He looked in our eyes and felt the
closeness and tenderness in both of us. So, he
negotiated a reasonable truce and Shechem, his
father, and all the men in their entourage were
circumcised. Then, came the treachery.

My brothers deceived us all. They were
treacherous and robbed me of a chance to marry my
love and find security in a loving relationship. They
were cruel, unjust and irrational. I feel as if
someone punched me in my gut. They made us
think if the men were all circumcised, then I would
be given to Shechem for his wife. We had not a
clue that the day they would be most sore during the
healing, my crazy brothers would take their lives'.

When Abah found out that my brothers
slaughtered innocent men in the night while they
could not protect themselves, he seemed disgusted

by their actions. Yet, his silence was reflective and cool spirited. His desire to act in a manner beneficial to both our family and the surrounding neighbors caused him to act quickly and critically to clean up my brother's disgraceful mess. And still, not one time, has anyone thought about me.

Now, my father Jacob has us packing our camels and running, again. Simeon and Levi's retaliation puts our family in jeopardy and makes peaceful coexistence impossible. Though Abah severely chided my brothers for their cowardice, he said we are headed for Bethel, the place of God, where he ran when Dod Esau chased him before any of us were born. He said we should always seek the God of his fathers' when we are in distress.

I still don't think he knows that my other Emah, or should I say my Dodah Rachel, is still hiding that strange idol she stole from Saba Laban's house when we fled. I saw her fondling it the night before; she didn't see me, but I saw her. Abah told us to leave all my Saba's idols where they were. Dodah Rachel had a hard time trusting in Abah's God, that was the difference between she and my Emah. Emah grew to believe in Him.

In each moment I breathe this story of love and violence. I need the women in my life to stop fighting and see I am grieving. I don't see why everyone is in distress. I am the one who was victimized. I'm the one who lost my love, I'll never be able to forget my Shechem and don't nobody care how I feel.

Abah rode alongside my camel for a while and talked to me about his God. He called Him Yah. Abah said Yah wanted to comfort me. He said Yah understood my pain and He knew my tears. I wanted to hug Abah for seeking me out to show empathy and compassion. I couldn't stop hurting. He said he wanted me to learn to seek his comfort from Yah.

"Walk with Yah like my Softah Sarah and my Emah Rebecca. Softah Sarah was faith filled and Emah Rebbecca was a sharp thinker. They were cunning, wailing women of prayer. They made Him their strength."

He told me how they walked with Yah, and in their walk with Him, they developed a lifestyle of praising Elohim. He said they made Yah their praise.

"They were intimate with Yah. The blessings they derived from such a close and intimate relationship with God brought healing, salvation and supernatural things into their lives. Angels spoke to Softah Sarah because of her intimacy with Yah."

Abah told me to just talk to Yah so I could learn to move a step further in my relationship with God every day. He explained that by making Him my praise, I would begin to see how Elohim would bring healing to my mind and body.

"He will also deliver you from the plans and attacks of the enemy because He is with you to heal and save you. Go through your day today knowing Yah is your praise," Abah explained while he comforted me.

"I've been so focused on my own problems I neglected to teach you to pray Dinah. I'm so sorry for my grave mistake. My word concerning their actions is that I refuse to accept any part of their vengeance. When we make camp at even, we can talk to Yah together, you have my word dear daughter."

I couldn't wait to get off that camel and hug him. After he smiled at me and told me he loved me, he left to check on the others.

"Next time, and there will be a next time, talk to me before making a decision about whom to give your affections," he whispered. *"Give me your word, daughter."*

"I give you my word Abah," I cried. My tears began to flow again, but this time, I began to talk to Yah as I cried. I needed His help. *"Heal me, O LORD, and I shall be healed; save me, and I shall be saved: for thou will become my praise,"* I prayed.

8

Healing Sprued Out

I

When it comes to you Lord, I'm limited
Here offering to you most willingly
tried to make peace with my brother as told
I'm grateful for having the mind to serve
Absolve me from hidden iniquity
Use me for what you desire me be
Look down on me I desire to toil
Sprue not me out of the race for my walk
Struggle so I won't be smoke in your nose
Great power in praying with a good heart
Within your boundaries my prayer is sweet
Heart is ready to be used for the good
For the Lion of the tribe of Judah
The God of Israel will vindicate me

II

Cannot hide from this rocky road I tread
My Lord and soul must come before my wed
Until now only sadness has been fed
Transform previous to put in my bed
By fruits of the spirit let him be led
Let him be most kind as the sword has said
Will submit to a benevolent head
Bless me because of your word I have read
I need love of the Most High God instead
Soon the damage from the words will be dead
Must two become more perfect for to wed
For my sin and others His blood was shed

I live by His holy word not just bread
Every knee shall bow as this word is spread

III
Saw them first at a young tender eighteen
Discovered world had never seen before
Submitted to change with tender kindness
Learned to fear and hate the monsters inside
Did not expect sting of the scorpion's tongue
Young mind so impressed by their charm and glare
Promised sweet tender love with passion flare
Words possess power to heal or to hurt
No slap no shove yet fierce words with mean stare
Stomach so tight when attacked and beat down
Like a knife in hands of skillful surgeon
Tiny tongue has power of life and death
Belittled confused promises broken
Was powerful pain in those words spoken

IV
Healing sprued out from the pouring rainstorm
The persecution God must now remove
Finally, she will not have to look back
They hurt her because she let them do it
The sting of the tongue can sting her no more
Yearned and desired a more kinder mate
Often wanted to lie down and take rest
Stumbled on healing power in writing
Woke up one day and felt the healing flow
That day pouring rain began to take shift
Healing power of the words from without
Words shook their sorrow then shattered their pain
Spirit brought choice words cause spirit knew them

Precious healing of mind spirit and soul

V

Open to me the windows of heaven
Let me abide under your hedges please
Rebuke the accusers for my own sake
Forgive me Lord of my transgressions too
Author and complete the faith I so need
All my sins are manifested to you
Take heed to self so you can make me new
I call on you in my time of sickness
Cast me not out but gather me to fold
Bless me according to my well doing
With all boldness I speak your Holy word
I glorify you for all you have done
I can do nothing without both of you
Jesus the father and Jesus the son

VI

Please don't tarry Lord come near unto me
I take my direction from you Most High
This is my time to wait upon you Lord
I fall on my knees and pray for your grace
I confess my sins and faults to your face
Wisdom me God in my time of sorrow
Your answers may come later or come now
Search my heart Jesus and correct me please
Cause not my mind to depart from your law
Let my healing flow from errors you saw
Let me do nothing through my vainglory
Let me do nothing through my hate or strife
I will not ask amiss from my own lusts
My ways acknowledge you and show my trust

VII

Jesus, I pray that you help me to stay
Meek humble merciful and pure in heart
Help me walk more perfect than yesterday
My desire is to follow your cue
You and only you will I seek to serve
I love you with all my heart soul and might
Remove pride from my heart so I can't fall
Make me whole so my members won't perish
Hold my tongue back from speaking ill of all
It becometh me to fulfill this quest
To live amongst your saints who are most true
Made perfect through your law this love is best
My faith remains intact trust remains stout
Am living by every word that proceed out

9

A Touch of Home

Through the phone wires, his voice stung as Aviel proudly proclaimed, *"that's how I met my wife."*

"Why is he talking to me about 'his wife'? I should have been the one he married! "What's wrong with me?" she wondered. "Why can't the men I love, love me in return? I deserve to be treated well; don't I? If not Aviel or my ex-husband, why can't I find someone to treat me like a queen? All I want is to love and be loved. Why doesn't any man think I am pretty enough? Why doesn't any man think I am smart enough? Why doesn't any man think I am worthy enough to be an adored wife?"

Maayan knew her sister saw Aviel the other day and gave him her number. She expected this phone call from her old flame, but this was not what she anticipated.

"Shalom Aleichem achoti, pretty lady. I heard about your divorce, is it finalized yet? I'm here if you need me," Aviel offered.

It was nice to know he was concerned even if he had ulterior motives, *"A lot has happened since I last saw you. How is life?",* she responded, in an attempt to change the subject.

"Life is good. I've missed you! I've grown a lot since we broke up."

Aviel was always frank about his feelings. He was a lady's man, and it was ultimately the reason their relationship ended. That was one thing for sure Maayan knew she couldn't deal with. He was into multiplying his love amongst beautiful women.

"I've been through trials and tribulations, and probably learned a lesson or two I wish I hadn't. Occasionally, I've thought about you as well. So, it's nice to hear your voice," she admitted.

But the truth was, she thought about him often, and even more so when her ex-husband was emotionally negligent.

"I heard through the grapevine you haven't been smiling much. You should let me change that. I always loved your smile," he added.

Maayan heard through the grapevine Aviel was single again. So, she was taken aback when he professed his love for his new wife. Her stomach twisted in knots, knowing he has married yet again. With her marriage dissolved, she had hoped for an opportunity to be the object of his affection again.

"Maybe this time you'll be a better husband." She didn't really mean it, but it was the right thing to say. *"Which one is this? Your third? Right?"* she stabbed, trying to ignore her own pain. *"Are you*

still in Texas? I heard you moved there with your second wife," Maayan added, twisting the knife a little deeper.

Her ears picked up his light snickering through the phone. Aviel was used to these kinds of passive-aggressive attacks. He faced it often from the women who found themselves tangled in his web of love.

"You know I can't be still for too long," Aviel joked. *"Adivah, my second wife couldn't deal with it either."*

Maayan knew exactly what that meant. Aviel had a gentle and kind approach, but his heart would always be divided.

"Do you remember Yaffa? She and I came to Chi-Town together for the summer."

Maayan interrupted *"Yes, I remember Yaffa, the woman who is not your wife?"* Stab!

Aviel sucked his teeth as if almost annoyed. *"Yes, Yaffa, the woman who is not my wife."* He continued. *"She came along to keep me company as I attended to some family business. But we will be heading back to Texas soon. You know I have to make that money in order to keep up with all my hunnys,"* he stabbed back. *"That's beside the point though. I can hardly wait to see you again in a beautiful summer dress. You know how I love a pretty lady sashaying around in a sundress*!*"*, he added trying to make love and not war.

"Is that supposed to be a compliment?", she asked sarcastically, trying to hide the fact she secretly enjoyed any and every compliment he gave her no matter how double handed it was.

"Yes, and I have more waiting for you if you play nice. I must admit it took me a minute to find your phone number; I misplaced it amongst my other numbers."

"Well, I see you found it."

"You know how persistent I am when I want something. Can I take you to lunch before I leave?"

She knew exactly what he meant. It seems she and Adivah walked away from Aviel for the same reason. Maayan began to notice this toxic cycle of them entertaining the same conversations as they dipped and dabbed in and out of each other's lives. She naively held on hoping Aviel would change. She hoped he would be more settled and loyal. And more than anything she hoped he was single.

"You know I will always love you; you will always be my first love," he swooned.

"You always have a warm place in my heart too Avee. But you know I am not the type of woman to infiltrate another sister's space," she proclaimed,

feeling slightly unsure of whether she was trying to convince herself or him.

She never envisioned after their last encounter eleven years ago that he'd be married, again! This was not a reality she welcomed. There was an ache in the pit of her stomach, the place where emotions lounge. Aviel always found her; she got a random call from him ever so often. These were calls she welcomed, no matter how unfruitful.

Like most young girls, Maayan wanted to be a loving and devoted wife. Often in her marriage, her heart would ache from not being touched by a warm and kind man. She often felt herself withering away because of her husband's constant detachment. She remembered feeling abandoned and rejected. This wasn't a feeling with which she could grow to be accustomed. A wife is supposed to be comforted and protected by her husband.

Over the years, she realized no matter the age, a woman perpetually loves when she is loved deeply. She felt imprisoned by the lack of companionship from her husband. The irony was she never wanted to be alone, yet she always felt alone even when he was laying in the bed next to her. She longed to be a loving and respectful wife. She earnestly desired to reap the love she diligently sowed.

Not a day went by when she didn't daydream about being a wife to a loving husband. Not a week went by when she didn't think about how she should respond to the kindness of a loving husband. Not a month went by when a tear did not fall from the wells of her eyes as her thoughts tried to bloom through the rocky soil her marriage was built upon.

Her passion drove her, like one of Langston Hughes' dreams deferred, a fantasy that would not be fulfilled.

She remembered the first time she laid eyes on Aviel years ago, in the South Shore High School auditorium. It was the last assembly, before winter break. He stood there, smiling at her from not far away. Maayan remembered how she caught his eye; she returned the smile and he received it as a welcome message. She could feel his smile permeate her; it reached in and touched her soul.

His smile was a warm, comfortable and tender touch; it marked her heart for life. It would never leave her because she didn't want to ever let it go. She felt at home with him. Her feet would not move; they were steadfast. They felt heavy and light at the same time. She did not want her legs to carry her away. His eyes set her heart ablaze. They reached her soul. She was helpless with no defense from his allure.

In the beginning, she was excited to feel him feeling her. She always felt vulnerable because, at the age of sixteen, Maayan's father was supposed to show her the love she sought from others. She needed the comfort of a strong man in her life. She needed the encouragement of a loving father to guide her and make her feel pretty. It was a critical thing; it could have protected her from the smile Aviel radiated her way that unforgettable day.

Though Maayan did have a father, he wasn't willing to be colored a real dad. He was not engaged in her life, which left her open and vulnerable. She needed love, and it seemed she was falling in love right there, in the auditorium, with this fine young man and his warm smile. Aviel's smile was not seductive. It invited her and made her trust him. He momentarily locked her into his grasp. It was only natural for her to respond with an unquestionable and an enthusiastic *"Yes!"* when Aviel asked, *"Will you give me a chance to love you?"*

She doesn't remember what happened to that comfort she interpreted at their first encounter. She couldn't remember where it went wrong when it went sour. In real life, love at first sight, is most often a recipe for disaster. Aviel and Maayan's story was no different. Maayan thought it would be one of those happily ever after stories like Cinderella. In the story, Prince Charming was a love possessed man searching high and low, day and night for the mysterious beauty with which he danced at the ball. Unbeknownst to him, his true love was squandering away as a mere servant girl. As the story is told, the day Cinderella's foot was made a match to the slipper was her moment of reckoning. But do we know what really happened? Did she really live happily ever after?

As Maayan thought back, she knew she should have been more cautious. Even after so many years, his eyes, his voice, and his touch burned intensely. She was defenseless as if in a crossfire. She remembered how disillusioned she was before as she tried to reconnect with his comforting smile and that initial spirit of trust that overtook her in the high school auditorium. That was what she longed for all these years. This is what she could never forget. This is what she could not stop feeling. This is what haunted her in her flawed marriage. This is what continued to haunt her now as she approached this new phase of her life.

As she stood in the auditorium, frozen and unable to move or speak, she never thought she'd be his star-crossed lover, destined to be a part of him, as he loved someone else over and over again. She remembered making love to him that laudable first time and then that wretched last time. She basked in the glory of feeling the arms of her lover again, when he stopped in mid-stroke to ask her, *"Who have you been sleeping with?"*

At that moment she forgot to enjoy his touch, to enjoy his smell, to enjoy being in his arms again. She began to grieve before the act was complete. She mourned as he walked her home. *"I'll never stop trying,"* she said to herself as she climbed those five stairs and he backed away from her reach. What caused this unsavory stench? Those words, *"I'll never stop trying,"* imbued her brain, they sketched a permanent scar across her heart. It was a mark that would haunt her for many years.

Part of her scarred heart would always belong to Aviel. It would always long for him. Like a drug, it would still yearn for that introductory sensation. That sensation that flowed through her and spread like the wings of a butterfly. She felt all this upon their first glance in the high school auditorium. Those feelings of comfort, trust, protection and love, would never leave her. Her memories would not go away. Instead, over time, they intensified and willed him in and out of her life. They haunted her with the uncertainty of what could have been, what she wished it were. What she feared it would never be. She could have been content there if he could commit his love solely to her.

Before their conversation on the phone ended, he offered to make her part of his life. He said he'd do it her way. He offered to keep it private, just between the two of them. But Maayan couldn't be anybody's secret life. So instead, he proposed to include her into his life slowly. He was confident he could get his wife to agree. But Maayan could not be responsible for breaking another sister's heart; becoming a sister wife was not her cup of tea. She wanted neither his pity, nor to be his pawn. Yet, she wanted him to hear her laugh so he wouldn't know how sad she really was. It was one of the most tragic and loneliest smiles she'd ever felt before. In an attempt to escape from his poisonous love, she concocted a story which required this unhealthy exchange to come to an end.

"Avee, it's been good talking to you, but I have to get off the phone."

"Hey, babe don't be like that. It's nothing but love. If you allow me, I can love you like no other. You know I'm the only one that can love you right!"

"Yea… It's been real, but I gotta go." She quickly said, *"Goodbye, Avee,"* and hung up before he could convince her otherwise.

After she hung up the receiver, she knew she had to hang up every desire and illicit thought she ever had about Aviel. She began to think about the man with whom she embarked on a marriage with. Where she lived in loneliness. She never understood why she was married and felt so alone. That marriage did not feel like home. She realized in her ignorance how her adulterous thoughts for Aviel began to deteriorate her marriage before it even started. She considered her husband a shack leaving her wanton for shelter and Aviel was the only shelter she desired.

Her thoughts caused her to feel somber, as tears ran down her face. *"Who will love me now? What's wrong with me? Did my hands help play the fiddle that led to its end and demise?"* The Dells song, *"The Love We Had Stays on My Mind"* played over and over again as she lay there thinking of Aviel and how she would never get a chance to be loved by him, to be touched by him, or to have him repossess her youth now gone and forgotten.

In each moment, she listened to the song and she felt more hopeless to this "dream deferred." She felt a surge of anger rise from the place where she stored her longing. She was not his helpmeet. He didn't choose her. She was not the one chosen to encourage him. She didn't get the joy of supporting his dreams. She was not his companion. It was not her pleasure to be his inspiration. She was not commissioned to help make him feel good about himself. She was not his mate.

Her obscure emotions constantly left her open and vulnerable. She had her moment of reckoning, when she realized she willed the keys to her freedom and all she had to do was simply move on. Maybe if she stopped hunting a ghost, she could have invested more energy in finding new love or making her marriage work.

Her toxic thoughts started again, *"How could he not know? How could he not feel me? Maybe he does know, but he clearly doesn't care?"*, she considered. *"How can I learn to stop being in love with a dream?"* She tried to muster up at least a soft smile for Aviel's happy life. She wondered how many times love could break the same heart. This would be the last time Maayan would accept one of these calls.

Maayan stopped the thoughts before they grew from anger to ugliness, which lies inside of bitterness. She needed to unearth the touch of home within herself. She was suddenly relieved at her fresh thoughts and felt renewed because, in the stillness of her mind, she quickly and silently called upon her Creator for help. *"Keep back thy servant also from presumptuous sins; let them not have dominion over me,"* she recalled the scripture prayed:

Father help my self-image.
Help me to find identity in you
understand my worth
value your standards
recognize my unique qualities designed by you
Lord, to you I pray

Help me to appreciate me
see myself the way you see me
understand that you Lord fashioned me too a
    little lower than the angels
view you as my author and designer
Lord, before you these things I lay

Help me to see you crowned me with glory and honor
to know you made me to have dominion over the
    creation as well
understand you put all things under my feet to boot
ask you to quiet the voice that whispers otherwise
seek your satisfaction and yours alone
Lord, I utter your praise today

Help me to hear your voice
taste your perfection
realize you will make my life successful
comprehend I have no power perceive real
realize all power is yours,
Father, give me ears to say

"Have mercy upon me, O God, according to thy
lovingkindness: according unto the multitude of
thy tender mercies blot out my transgressions.
Wash me throughly from mine iniquity, and
cleanse me from my sin. For I acknowledge my
transgressions: and my sin is ever before me.
Against thee, thee only, have I sinned, and done
this evil in thy sight: that thou mightest be
justified when thou speakest, and be clear when
thou judgest."

In that instance she learned she needed to love herself; find comfort and solace in the one who created her. At that moment she knew her happiness was not tied to the love of any man. She realized her happiness was tied to The Most High and at last she was done.

10

Fragrance of Love

My husband is the father of many nations as prophesied. Yah showed me in a dream he would be revered among Israelites, Edomites, Muslims, and Christians worldwide for generations to come. In this dream, I saw he would be the progenitor of Shem, the father of all Semitic people and cultures. He was a faithful man whom I respected long before I fell in love with him. I bore my husband six sons. My respect for him grew every day as I witnessed him show kindness to others around us.

I have nothing but honor and admiration for Sarah as well. As her handmaiden, I knew her well; she was my longtime friend, and I was her confidant. Sarah taught me how to pray; this was one of the greatest gifts she imparted to me. I comforted her in her last days and attended to her every need. Because I was a constant presence in their lives, people began to speculate I had become Abraham's concubine while Sarah was alive. But, because of my admiration for her, I won't attest whether or not I ever touched her husband and he ever touched me while Sarah was still alive.

Abraham and I fell in love after he saw how tenderly I cared for Sarah. After she saw our connection develop, she gave us her blessings. Sarah loved Abraham with all her heart. Not wanting him to be alone or feel guilty; she facilitated a relationship between us, which eventually blossomed.

I watched how Hagar, the Egyptian handmaiden, and Ishmael, her son, disrespected Sarah and her son Isaac. I knew that was a grave mistake. Though God blessed her womb, Hagar didn't grow in the fruit of the spirit. Instead, she became insolent. After she got pregnant, Hagar segregated herself from the sisterhood Sarah worked so hard to build. Whether Hagar's pride in her pregnancy was subtle or overt, Sarah picked up on it immediately, and she didn't like it. Hagar thought she was better than everyone else. Here this woman invites you into her home to bear children for such a faithful man as Abraham, with no regard for herself or her feelings, and you show your true colors? Hmph!

Hagar's illicit behavior continued after Ishmael was born. She refused to teach him how to love and respect his brother. This was part of her downfall. God established Sarah as Abraham's first wife; she was the one whom He chose to carry the seed who would inherit the birthright. Hagar failed to understand that! Even if Isaac was chosen to carry the birthright, it did not mean God was not omnipotent enough to ensure all our sons would be blessed. I tried to remind Hagar, but she didn't listen. Obviously, she wasn't the sharpest tool, nor the wisest of women. She had the audacity to despise Sarah and look at her with contempt just because Sarah could not bear Abraham a child.

Hagar provoked Sarah until she could bear no more. Sarah told Abraham to rid us of Hagar's wickedness. Hagar must have forgotten she was only the surrogate. She did not remember Sarah chose her, not Abraham. My heart was broken that day; I was hoping it would never come to that point.

Had Hagar considered, she could have contemplated that God would not object to her being expelled from the camp. Regardless of the nation from which we came, as members of Abraham's household, we were mandated to serve The Most High. We were all obligated to learn more about the eternal Elohim every day. It became natural for us to pray and build our trust in Him. Yet and still, Hagar had to learn the hard way.

I remember how livid Abraham was, as he reminded Hagar constantly to circumcise Ishmael; she knew that was a rule of the house. Her slothful attitude almost cost Ishmael his life. If it weren't for Abraham's steadfastness, Hagar would have broken the covenant, which is why Abraham circumcised Ishmael himself at the age of thirteen. Hagar was one disobedient woman. I don't know why she thought Abraham would love her more than he loved Sarah or God's commandments. I tried to warn her, but the poor thing was just confused.

As Sarah and Hagar's relationship continued to disintegrate; it became apparent to everyone Abraham wanted nothing to do with the whole situation. He only conceded in the first place because Sarah insisted. In her lack of faith, Sarah couldn't see the promise to come; the only way she fathomed "obtaining children" was by her Egyptian servant girl. As things continued to spiral out of control, Sarah confided in me. Choosing Hagar was a mistake; she only wanted to fulfill God's promise.

One day, Sarah watched Ishmael taunt Isaac while Hagar candidly sat by watching. That was the straw that broke the camel's back. We were stunned when Sarah laid hands on Hagar. My mouth hung open. I knew Sarah; she was humble, kind, and meek, but that day all fruit of the spirit flew out the window. Sarah slapped Hagar senseless.

The other handmaidens and I tried to warn Hagar; she was getting too arrogant and headed down the wrong path. Still, she wouldn't listen. Sarah was not a jealous woman; but Hagar provoked her constantly. We all thought Hagar's behavior was deleterious. There was nothing Godly about it. Sarah tried to be patient before she made Abraham put her out. It didn't take long for Hagar to learn her place and see the error in her ways.

You could say I learned from Hagar too. I learned what not to do if I didn't want Sarah to lay hands on me. Hagar's expulsion was the talk of the camp, and some people thought Abraham was being unjust when he put the girl out with not enough rations for her journey. Abraham was certainly caught in the middle of a situation. What was he supposed to do? He didn't want to know what was going on with the women, so he did nothing—like most men.

Abraham didn't want to deal with it, he gave Hagar no added attention and no extra energy. He never tried to force Hagar into submission, and he let her hang herself. Why should he have to inflict pain upon her anyway? She did the job his wife asked her to do; she got pregnant. Her job was done, Hagar was Sarah's handmaid, so he let her handle it. But that wasn't enough for Sarah, because Hagar kept provoking her, he was too passive about the entire situation, so Sarah told him what to do, what she thought was best!

You can't make this stuff up. But, in hindsight, maybe had Abraham been more proactive, this entire situation may never have transpired. His inactivity was the reason Hagar felt comfortable mocking Sarah. You should have seen Hagar's smirk drop when Abraham quieted his wife's rage. In the beginning Abraham was reluctant, until the Most High stepped in. I was the one who heard

Sarah's prayers every morning as I tended to her needs. I heard her praying for the best on behalf of her family, including Hagar.

When Hagar returned from expulsion, she was a changed woman. We could tell she learned to listen to the voice of The Most High. She elaborated to me how difficult it was for her in the desert. First of all, why in the heck did she walk towards the desert anyway, especially knowing she had limited rations? She should have walked in the opposite direction, where she would have found vegetation and water. That showed me how many screws were really loose in Hagar's head. It would have taken longer, but the land would have provided for her until she got to Egypt. Her saving grace was Ishmael. The Most High heard the lad's cry and put his hedges of protection around them, keeping them safe until they returned to us.

God sometimes calls us to account for our inappropriate behavior in our wanderings from His perfect will. Hagar's time in the desert was her opportunity to fully understand the faith Abraham and Sarah tried to impart to her. In the end, it all worked out. Sarah forgave Hagar; she did not mistreat her, but she would not trust her again. Hagar remained in the shadows after that. I felt sorry for her.

In her later days, I grew closer to Sarah and served her well. I learned everything I could from her. She was a virtuous woman; up early looking well to the needs of her household and teaching us to be submissive and cunning in prayer. Sarah died with no daughters, but she had many handmaidens. Every day she gathered us for prayer and worship.

On the Shabbat eve she invited us into her tent for bread and wine. Those were good times, and we had so much fun. We talked about everything and laughed a lot. She encouraged sisterhood, and she taught us to love each other as we learned the ways of Abraham's God and built our faith in Him. Every night she prayed for each of us. I listened to her pray for her husband and her son at least three times every day until the day she gave up the ghost.

Once Sarah died, Abraham commissioned a team of men servants to escort Hagar and Ishmael to her homeland, where she would be happier. By then, Hagar understood her son would become many nations too as The Most High promised Abraham. In Egypt, Ishmael took a wife and started his own family having twelve sons. As a promise to Sarah, Abraham vowed Isaac would live in peace as the only son. Which meant when his other sons came of age, Abraham sent them away, but he did not let them leave empty-handed; he sent them away with a substantial inheritance. He wanted them to be men of wealth and standards. He wanted them esteemed in the lands where they decided to dwell.

11

The Enemy Within

A Woman's Prayer of Hope

Now I lay me down to sleep
My faith in Yah I hope to keep
Filled with hurt instilled down deep
Filled with all the victories I reap
A careful blend of life's many spices
Walking the straight and narrow avoiding Satan's devices
Turning away from all evil entices
Obedience is better than any sacrifices
If I should die before I wake
I pray for forgiveness of any mistake
Seeking New Jerusalem and escaping the lake
Save me Father for your name's sake
Guide my husband, as he is my head
Leading with benevolence as your word said
Now I lay me down to rest
I pray that I have passed my test
Bless my children from any heartache
Bless them Jesus so they too may partake
Now I lay me down to sleep
Comfort me Yahuah so no longer I weep
If I should die before I wake
Into your kingdom me please take.

I hope nobody will ever have to look at anybody they love through the eyes of an evil spirit. As a hoary-haired woman in the winter years of life, I look back on my journey from a young wife to a widow laughing and crying at the same time. Have you ever literally laughed and cried at the same time? I don't mean have you ever laughed until you cried. I mean laughed AND cried at the same time. I laugh because I feel peace and joy that passes all understanding, I feel as if I am living that scripture. I have never been happier in my life.

My childhood was full of struggles. I watched my parents argue ferociously; I watched my mother struggle to feed us with no help from my father. I watched my father bring my brother a shining new bike for my little sister's birthday. I listened to my aunt and uncle, who lived with us, say vile and horrendous things to one another in anger. I am free from the evil that spewed from my own husband's mouth as he recited Isaiah 3:16-26. He knew it word for word, he emphasized every punctuation in his tone. The scowl on his face and his body language were as the countenance of an evil spirit as he said to me, "Because the daughters *of Zion are haughty…" The words no longer ring in my ear. I can't hear it anymore, it wasn't me in the first place, and it never will be me.*

I used to think my husband hated me, but looking back, I realize I was fighting an evil spirit in him that he himself did not know how to fight. I look back and find peace. Our heavenly Father knows best, so I hope the good my husband did for others in his life will outweigh the evil he caused us, his wife and children. I forgive him completely for his hatred against me and my children.

I know fully the meaning of Yeshuah's prayer as he hung on the cross, "Father forgive them for they know not what they do." I'm not as good as my Messiah, so I could never fully understand this type of forgiveness. But with understanding, I can easily forgive. I have peace in my new home, my last home. My spirit is quieted, I only hear my thoughts and the worship songs ringing from Spotify on my Smartphone. I feel relief from the sadness of being a rejected wife.

I still cry though, because I feel sad my sons have never had a loving father to guide them and teach them how to be men. They struggle learning to be kind and loving men because they didn't see that in their father. He could not be their example. He was an example of how NOT to treat your wife and children. My daughter has never had a father to be her first love, to show her how a man is supposed to love her. She has never been a daddy's girl. *Every girl should know how that feels. I also cry because I have never experienced being loved by a man. My husband could not render unto the wife due benevolence, the evil spirit within him would not allow him to do it. He was the monster under our beds who terrorized us more than he loved us through his actions.*

What used to confuse me is how he could show so much compassion to other women whose husbands abused them emotionally. I could never understand how the people at the church where we served spoke of him with such honor and respect and so much love. As I watched him perform in the house of prayer, I marveled at what I thought was hypocrisy. When in fact, my husband was actually a good man, a strong man with an acumen for The Word of God like few other men. He was a man deserving respect. At home though, this was rarely the man we experienced. As I think about it, I realize he was literally fighting an evil spirit for his life.

In each moment, as I think about these facts, a single drop of water falls from the tear ducts of each eye. This is good progress because in my youth, I wailed at the thoughts of being a wife rejected. I feared. I felt ashamed and confounded. I felt as if I was forced to live in shame. As a young wife, I never thought I could ever forget the shame of my youth. I was not a widow then, but I still felt the reproach of widowhood, because I lived as if I walked on eggshells every day of my life. I wanted to crave his touch, his voice, his kiss, and his presence, but he didn't offer much of that. He wasn't a touchy-feely kind of guy, unless it was time to copulate; his goal was to show his manliness and skill; all I wanted to do was make love. So, I always felt starved.

My youth was stolen by this evil spirit I did not know existed. I laid in bed with the enemy that was within him for twenty-one years of my life. Still, I could not understand the enemy and how to fight IT, until I found the strength and resources within myself to remove me and my children from its midst. I learned a lot about spiritual warfare over the years, so I know everything I did back then was wrong.

I wasn't born Simchah. It is a Hebrew name, it means Joy; rejoice at heart; spiritual joy. That is the name I chose for myself. Tobiah, my husband, decided my name should be Tamar. It is biblical, from the book of Genesis, she was the wife of Er, Judah's first-born son, and he liked her story. Though I preferred Simchah, he called me Tamar throughout most of our marriage. I was born Paula, named after my father Paul. Paula, no special meaning, no eloquent significance, no expressive interpretation, just Paula.

I am Simchah, a virtuous and praying woman, a cunning, wailing woman of prayer, busy taking care of the needs of my family. I am teaching my daughter to fight spiritual warfare with praise. I am teaching my daughter and her daughter how to pray.

Simchah smiled after re-reading her final paragraph. She slowly closed the journal and lovingly caressed the cover before easing the leather-bound book into the small chest on the table in front of her. *Drip. Drip.* A single tear fell from each of her eyes as she thought about all the years of blood, sweat and tears that went into filling the pages of those seven journals. Though she knew the battle was never hers to begin with, because the battle belongs to the Lord, she felt a since of victory and completion. Simchah felt like she had finally made it to the finish line. She knew the race was given to those who endured until the end. Her thoughts were interrupted by the sweet sounds of her granddaughter's voice.

"Softah" shouted Zaharah. *"Sister Joanna is calling you. Should I answer your phone? Do you want me to bring it to you?"*

"No, I'll call her back when I finish sewing the bodice onto my dress. I'm planning on wearing it to Chag Shavuot, and I really want to finish this today," Simchah shouted back.

As Zaharah came into the sewing room, she laid the phone on the cutting table near the sewing machine so Simchah could reach it.

"It gives me great pleasure to dress up for The Lord for the feast of weeks. Plus, the dress I wore for the last feast day is too tight, so I have a good excuse to make myself something new for this feast."

"You know she's going to blow up your phone until you answer, right?" reminded Zaharah. *"She wants you to sit with Saba while she hits the streets with her good time girls!"*

"What do you know about a good time girl?" questioned Softah.

"I hear about Sister Joanna at Bible class when I'm home from school," admitted Zaharah. *"I don't understand how you could keep helping her anyway. Saba is not your responsibility any longer. He left you over 20 years ago and he don't even know you anymore. Why haven't you married again anyway? He did and it didn't take him long either."*

"First of all, Saba didn't leave me. I removed myself because I was fed up with being accused! I was tired of weeping and thinking of myself as a victim. I made a choice for your Emah and your uncles; my daughter and sons. I chose to separate from Saba. Second, the scripture says I will be his wife until one of us dies. Even though he has another wife and even though he has been battling Alzheimer's for the past eight years, Saba is not dead yet. Third, I know you will be twenty-one in a few months, but you need to stay out of grown folks' business. You will never be grown enough to disrespect me or your Saba!"

"I'm sorry Softah. I did not mean to be disrespectful."

"And furthermore, what are you doing to please Yah? Does your good outweigh your bad? You need to be working on that dear heart."

"Yeah, yeah, that's what you always say," retorted Zaharah, as Simchah frowned with displeasure.

"And whether you want to accept her or not, Sister Joanna is his wife, so she's also your Softah. What you need to be doing is watching that young man you're courting to make sure he's a good choice. I overheard your sweet nothings last night when you talked to him on the phone. You know the mistakes I made; don't you make the same ones. Now let me finish my dress in peace."

"Ok? Wait...What! Were you eavesdropping on me last night?" Zaharah protested with a pout. *"Softah, I may never be the woman you are. I don't think I can ever be prepared for that kind of womanhood. She will always be sister Joanna to me, she'll never be Softah. That's a title I reserve only for you, just for the record,"* she confided with a smile.

"Oh, and when can I interview you for my final project on domestic violence. My paper is due two weeks after spring break, and you are my last interview. I want to submit it early so I can wrap my mind around my senior year. I'm going back to campus in 3 days. Before I ask questions, I want to give you time to just tell your story."

Simchah sighed and nodded at her granddaughter. She picked up the small wood and leather treasure chest and pulled out one of the leather-bound books. It was worn around the corners and edges, and the pages were darkened from many years and many tears. Simchah handed the book and then the small chest filled with the other six journals to Zaharah and smiled.

"Zaharah, I have been living my story every single day of my life for decades. The words on these pages amount to more than just a project or a paper. These words give voice to my struggle and give praise to The Most High Yah who delivered me. Just read with an open mind and an open heart. I am sure you will find my story and a whole lot more than you bargained for on the tear-stained pages of this book. We can talk again, after you finish reading."

I spent many years being embarrassed to tell others my Bible teaching husband was a cruel, emotional abuser. I never told anyone the children ran to their rooms when they heard their father's key in the door each evening, because they feared his moodiness and never knew which mood he might be in when he came home. My children and I were happiest when my husband wasn't home, and no one minded his lateness at all. We actually

preferred it. I think it was so easy for him to be cruel because he really believed my only function in his life was in the kitchen and bedroom. He actually said that to my mother years ago.

"I only need her for the bedroom and kitchen," Drip. Drip.

Those were my husband's exact words to my mother. I was humiliated, but not enough to leave him alone, because I had already given my body to him to wife and I feared the wrath of God. My mother cried and feared for my happiness.

My mother warned me: "He'll throw you away like a dirty dish rag".

Those were her exact words, but being the stupid young woman I was, I told her she had no need to fear because he was a man of God, he used the Bible to guide his life so he was bound to change his mind and learn to treat me with benevolence. Man, was I wrong! It never changed. Tobiah never learned to treat me with the love and kindness. The only time he was gentle with me was during sex. As a matter of fact, he rarely touched me unless he wanted sex. Drip.
I wanted to walk away but feared I couldn't take care of the children alone; and I was afraid the sky would fall on me, because The Most High hates putting away. I was afraid I'd spent so much time living in fear and in emotional turmoil at the mouth of my husband that my aged smile, wrinkled eyes,

and saggy flesh would be the cause of no other man ever wanting me to wife. I feared being alone more than I feared the cruelty of his scorpion tongue when he walked in the door each evening. Tobiah also told me he couldn't be a father to our baby boy Nehemiah if I ever left him. What kind of crazy thought was that? What do you mean you can't be a father to our son if I leave you? I didn't think he was serious. I thought it was just another control tactic.

Two things gave me the courage to conquer my fears. First, the experience of my oldest son weeping on his high school graduation night gave me the courage to leave. His father accused him of lying and called him a lying dog as he railed on him and slashed his flesh with his scorpion tongue. My boy began throwing his belongings into a garbage bag so he could leave, with no place to go. He was going to run to a friend's home to stay with him and his parents. As I comforted him and begged him not to leave, I promised if he would allow me to help him get to his first year of college, when he came home for the first break, he'd come to a new home. I promised him I would leave his father to be in a safer place and I apologized for having him in such an environment for so long.

There was no evidence of the scorpion's tongue on our first dates; there were no red flags to alert me. Tobiah wooed me. He was gentlemanly and

kind. He opened doors for me, and only gentleness
came from his tongue. Abusive marriages rarely
start with abuse. In fact, our first dates were
probably pretty similar to those of most loving
couples. Tobiah was charming, he paid attention to
me, and he flattered me. His intelligence and his
gentleness attracted me. I was just a babe, naive
and wanting. I wanted what every young girl
wanted, to live a fairy tale. I prayed for a man who
knew the truth so I could follow him into the
kingdom of God. I wanted a husband who could
teach and lead me. One day, after Shabbat, Tobiah
declared The Most High told him I was his wife, I
was sent from Him. I believed he was the answer to
my prayers.

Our marriage was not conventional. The
minister at the Knesset we attended in those days
was a zealot. He needed to control his followers.
He told Tobiah it was time for us to get baptized,
then married. Tobiah told me, and I submitted. I
wanted to be a submissive and dutiful woman of
God. We were baptized one week, and for the first
ten years of our relationship we were married
according to Hebrew law. Our family and friends
were not invited.

We did not have a legal marriage license, so it
was our vow we said to one another on a random
Sabbath after Bible class which kept him with a
woman who he was sure was a whore. The vow
kept me tied to a man who had no trust in me at all,
one who admitted he didn't need me for anything
except to cook his food and satisfy him in bed yet
accused me of being disloyal and whorish over and

over again. It was his devaluing of me as a woman of God which made it easy for him to use his scorpion tongue to lash out at me so often. Drip.

At the end of the day, on the way to announce the marriage to my family, Tobiah revealed, "The Most High told me marrying you was a mistake."

He was not reluctant about his revelation. I didn't see that coming at all since he said the Father told him I was to be his wife. Drip. Drip. The next day, I was his lady, I was his dream, I was his wife, whom he SAID he loved, but there was no apology for crushing my feelings.

The accusation of adultery and the spirit of jealousy actually started very early in our relationship. In the beginning, I was stupid enough to think it was love. I thought it was flattering. The first time was when he accused me of looking at another young man in the church with wanton eyes. I comforted him with loving eyes, I grasped his hand gently and kissed him to reassure him that my eyes were 'wanton' only for him. But it only convinced him for the moment. There was always another time. It never stopped. Drip. I was accused of sleeping with the neighbor and his son,

116

the mail cashier, the gentlemen who owned the dance studio where I took exercise classes, the bus driver, the UPS man or the mailman. Drip.

Once I invited a friend from college, whom I had introduced to The Word, to spend the weekend for the Feast of Tabernacles. I made sure it was okay with my husband first, of course. He said yes and seemed to like the idea of me having a sister friend. As I prepared a space to make her comfortable, I noticed he watched me. While I entertained her during her visit, I noticed he watched me. When she left from what I thought was a really fun and festive feast weekend, he asked me a very strange question.

"Have you ever thought of having sex with a woman?" Drip.

I stared at him hesitantly, because I had no idea where this line of questioning was going. I chose to keep my response simple.

"No", I proclaimed firmly. "Why do you ask?"

"Because you seemed to go all out to make your girlfriend comfortable," he spat in an accusatory tone.

I did not appreciate the accusation and I chose not to respond. Then he asked, "Who molested you as a child? Was it one of your uncles or your father?"

I just walked away, into the back of the house to clean up after the festive feast weekend. Later, as we laid down for the night he declared, "We need to pray this spirit of illicit sex out of you. It is an evil spirit and we can be rid of it through fasting and prayer." Drip. Drip.

I looked at the ceiling when I responded, because I couldn't lock eyes with him at that moment:

"I will not pray a lie. I will not pray for a spirit of illicit sex to be prayed out of me that does not exist. It is a lie, so no. Absolutely no, I will not pray that prayer with you."

Then, I rolled over to face the wall feeling disgusted. I silently wept until I fell sleep. I felt embarrassed and unclean. I allowed myself to be isolated from the companionship of my friend, to avoid such a vile accusation. Drip. Drip.

Later that day, I was his wife, whom he SAID he loved, but there was no apology for accusing the men in my family of such atrocities.

Me: "Can women have male friends?"

Him: "No stupid."

Drip.

Me: "You don't believe men and women can have a platonic friendship? Have you ever had a female friend? Do you have one now?"

Him: "Whores want friendship with a man who penetrated them before so that when her husband disappoints her, she can be with him, and she doesn't feel like a complete whore, since he'd already been there."

Me: "I hadn't thought of it like that before."

Him: "Hadn't you?"

Me: "You can neither read nor change my thoughts. I was just trying to start a decent conversation."

Him: "How can I have a decent conversation with an indecent woman."

His voice was quiet, calm and calculated. His tone almost made me forget it was just another accusation. Drip.

I should have known better but Tobiah's sister's husband, David. called to ask if he could bring their three children to our house because the lights were out in their neighborhood from a storm. He said ComEd reported it would be late in the evening

before the power was restored. The children were 8, 5 and 2. David's wife, Marsha and Tobiah were both at work because it was early in the day. As a servant of God, I knew my role was to serve others and I honestly saw this as an opportunity to serve, so I said yes.

When they arrived, I set them up in the living room where the TV and VCR were, so they could be comfortable. I remained in the back of the house with no contact outside of bringing in popcorn and beverages occasionally. My own two-year old played with his children in the front of the house. I stuck my head in from time to time to check to make sure he was being a good boy. The two 2-year olds fell asleep on the floor after they enjoyed the lunch, I prepared for everyone. So, I went into the living room again to put both of them in one of the bedrooms where they could be more comfortable as they napped. Tobiah, stormed into the back door about 3 pm, looked at me angrily, as I sat in the little sewing-area I made for myself in the room off the kitchen. He walked to the front of the house in a rage.

"Nigger get out of my house! Don't ever come to my house again," he yelled at his brother-in-law. "I'm not stupid, nigga. You got a lot of nerve sleeping with my wife and stepping your feet in my house," he screamed as he squinted his eyes in a jealous rage.

All I heard my brother-in-law say was, "Tobiah! Man. What?"

*"You heard me nigga!" my husband retorted
sternly.*

*Drip. I was stunned. I was in shock as this
innocent man gathered his children and their things
quickly. I was utterly humiliated. Then, my
husband walked to the back of the house where I
stood in shock unable to move. My eyes locked eyes
with his as I waited for him to attack me.*

*"Don't you ever bring your nigga in my house
again. You have come to an all-time low, bringing
one of your niggas in my house with my son!"*

*Then, he stormed out the back door to the garage
where he did side work as an auto mechanic.
Tobiah swooped out as fast as he came in. And me,
I didn't know what to say, so I chose to say nothing.
Drip. Drip.*

*"The scriptures say if an unbelieving spouse walked
away for a better life and has no desire to return,
then let them go. I would welcome a bill of
divorcement at this point." I wanted him to make it
fit. He believed I was a whorish wife, which had to
mean I was an unbeliever right? "Then, I would
welcome a bill of divorcement at this point, since I
am blatantly disrespectful and just plain nasty." I
spoke softly to myself. At bedtime, I was his wife
again and we had sex throughout the night as he
whispered in my ear, "You have this stiff cock ready
for you anytime you want it. You never have to get
it anywhere else." Drip. Drip. Drip.*

121

I was cooking dinner and he came quietly in the back door from his auto shop in the garage. This time he grabbed my hand and led me to the bedroom. He laid me on the bed and began to raise my dress and remove my panties. I thought he just wanted a "quickie", so I responded favorably so as not to deny my husband. But he didn't want sex, he checked my vagina for semen, to see if I'd had sex while he worked. The problem was he believed it.

"Who was here today?", Tobiah asked in an accusatory tone. Drip.

"Only Odeliyah from Bible class. She brought by a few dresses she wanted me to alter for her. See?", I pointed to the dresses on my sewing table.

"Who else was here?" he interrogated.

"Nobody," in a defensive tone.

"Which one of your niggas did you have in my house?", he countered.

According to Tobiah, he dug for semen in my vagina and found it. At least that is what he told the minister when he brought me before the tiny church with charges of adultery. They discussed the woman in Numbers who was given poison. They

*discussed how to "handle" my whoredom. The
ritual of jealousy in Numbers 5:11-31 is a law that
both intrigued me and disturbed me. The bad thing
is that as they discussed this whorish wife, I
considered buying into it. I considered cooperating
and having my moment where I would once and for
all be vindicated and cleared of these horrendous
charges. This law perplexed me as well. I had read
it many times. It was the Word of God and I did
believe it wholeheartedly, but can I trust these two
men? Are they true men of God, does He listen to
them? Will He clear me of this charge? Was I
regarding the law or these two men as if it were
some bizarre and ridiculous process lying
somewhere between faith, stupidity or being
humiliated?*

*I knew this was it, I knew he'd give me a bill of
divorcement for sure this time. If he truly believed
it, then why would he want to stay married to a
whorish woman? Why wouldn't he put me away?
I wasn't sure how I felt about it. I got up and
walked home weeping. Drip. Drip.*

*The emotional abuse I experienced takes time to
build. It was slow, methodical and incessant, much
like a dripping kitchen faucet. In the beginning was
like a little drip I didn't notice. It mirrored an off-
hand remark that was, "just a joke." He told me I*

was too sensitive, and his remark was no big deal. It seemed so small and insignificant at the time.

"I am probably a little too sensitive," I repeated to myself. Drip.

I enjoyed my time alone in the house with my son watching him play and doing my duty as a wife. I read while he napped and kept my tiny garden as he ran in the yard. I thought about how I could learn to negotiate my own life in secret since I was married to a man who would not enable his wife to do great things besides make babies and cook his food. I did not sign up to be imprisoned and treated like a disdained wife.

Black people have been so busy fighting white supremacy that we did not see sexual terrorism in our own homes and communities. We've seemed to use every weapon in our arsenal to protect ourselves against racism and have not held abusive husbands accountable. My grandfather, who fled the south in The Great Migration, experienced the civil rights movement in all its' glory with the marching, bitten by dogs, water hoses, sit- ins, lynchings, and Jim Crow. He would have never believed his granddaughter would fear her husband and his evil rages and the misogynistic imbalanced system of marriage, because he treated my grandmother with benevolence. He didn't look at her submission to him as a weakness or an opportunity to put his foot on her neck, so she'd fear him.

"Am I in a righteous marriage or was my grandmother?" I often screamed in my head.

My grandmother was happy when my grandfather walked in the door after a hard day's work. She missed him. Her greatest peace was when he came home. The fact that my peace came while I was alone, while Tobiah was away from the house, should have been my clue.

I was going in and out of the basement on a really hot summer day in Chicago, to retrieve the laundry from the washer and hang it on the line in the yard to dry. While waiting for the last spin to stop, I noticed a telephone cord running along the top of the wall and going into a piece of the wall I now realized was a door. In the year we lived in the house I did not know there was another room in the basement. There was no doorknob and the door looked just like the wall, it blended right into it.

I managed to open the door and saw the phone cord was attached to another telephone and the telephone was attached to a cassette recorder. I noticed a cassette in the recorder and pushed play. To my astonishment, I heard a telephone call I had with my mother the previous night. I realized my husband tapped our phone. He was recording my conversations.

I saw other tapes with dates six months back and labels in a small box on the other side of the phone:

> *"w/her mother" ...*
> *"w/her sister" ...*
> *"w/Leah" ...*

125

"w/Brenda" ...
"w/Odeliyah" ...""
"w/me" (dated)...

There were 3 "w/me" with dates on them tapes.

"So, was he listening back at the conversations he and I have over the phone and analyzing them?", I asked myself. "Hmmmmm, why? This cannot be normal, do all husbands do this? Do all wives feel this way?", I asked myself through my tears. There were no tapes labeled Tobiah w/so and so...Why hadn't he heard I had nothing to hide yet? Drip.

If it is unlawful for a man to divorce his wife for any reason then because I am a mere woman, I did not think I stood a chance by pleading my cause to The Most High. Afterall, Tobiah had never put a hand on me, but his scorpion tongue was all over my soul stinging salacious words all over me. Drip. Drip.

Tobiah was really great at finding Bible quotes to back up his belief that God regarded men more highly than women and he didn't mind sharing them with me in front of my family and friends. He didn't mind letting me know he was always right, and I was always wrong. Not only was I wrong, but I was also haughty, walking with my head held high with my seductive eyes, prancing along, jingling my ankle bracelets, which I liked to wear.

When I go grocery shopping, I like to walk down each aisle one by one. Even though I always have a grocery list to ensure I get everything I need most, walking up and down each aisle to see what is available or what is in season is relaxing. As I walked down the aisle of the grocery store, a gentleman I'd never seen before stopped me in the produce section, as I took my time to fill a bag with semi-soft peaches.

"I recognize you," he said.

I looked to see if my husband was in earshot and eyesight. Tobiah was on the other side picking out pears, he loved pears. Drip.

"I have something for you" the stranger said. "I will be right back."

My stomach felt as if there were knots in it. I didn't move for a few minutes. Then I selected two more peaches, put them in the bag, placed the bag in the cart and met my husband at the pears.

"Who was that?" Tobiah asked.

"I don't know, I've never seen him before," I replied.

"What did he say to you?" Tobiah reviled.

"He asked how to select a good peach," I lied.

Then we headed down the rice and pasta isle. I wanted to find brown Jasmine rice and try a new recipe. Tia Curry Rice. Next, the seasoning aisle.

"There you are," said the strange man as he found me again. "I said I have something for you."

He then handed me my driver's license I lost a little over a year ago. I had since got a new one. "Thank you," I said confusingly as I grabbed my license from his hand and tried to make sure I didn't touch him.

"I found it outside the Walgreens on 75th street. I meant to drop it in the mailbox, but I kept forgetting."

"Thanks again," I said awkwardly.

I didn't want to appear rude, but how this kind stranger viewed me was of no importance at this awkward moment. I wondered how he recognized me in the store from an ID he has had in his car for more than a year. I had many questions which I knew I could not ask because my husband stood there with his hand on the cart watching my interaction with this stranger. The remainder of our time shopping was quiet. I didn't know how to start a conversation about the encounter because I

128

didn't have any answers and I knew questions were brewing in my husband's head.

"You said he asked about picking peaches," he knew I lied. I knew I shouldn't have lied. Drip.

"I didn't want to alarm you." I said. I was sorry, I knew I should not let his jealous rages cause me to lie.

"You are a liar. What else have you lied about?", Tobiah snarled.

"So, you left your driver's license in your lover's car huh?", he reviled. Drip. Drip.

I wasn't sure whether it was a question or a declaration.

"You heard him say he found it outside of Walgreens, remember? I had no idea where I lost it, remember?", I reminded him.

"How did he recognize you from your ID?", he asked.

"I have no idea," I responded uncomfortably. "I thought it was strange too, let's talk about it."

"You think I'm the one stupid," argued Tobiah.

I did not weep. As he railed me, I reviled back. Drip.

I never wanted to be the kind of woman to run back and forth or in and out of a relationship. I married Tobiah with the intention of being married for a lifetime. No matter what. My daily prayer was for God to strengthen me so I could. Thinking back, I should have been praying for a way out of this madness.

It had been two weeks since Tobiah touched me. He tried hard not to talk to me. I knew something was up, his silence was the result of another jealous episode.

Drip. Drip.

I declined to ask him who the culprit was this time. Tobiah waited for me to ask why he was angry, but I didn't. We'd been here before and I knew the outcome would leave me in tears again. This was the first time I thought of leaving, but the prophet Malachi said God hates putting away. So, I prayed for God to make me stronger, to take the hard times, to endure until things got better. Is that not what a submissive wife is supposed to do for salvation?

Two days later, we were laughing and having a good time as we watched television and just enjoyed each other's company. I loved my husband's humble spirit at these times. This person, whom I loved to be in his company, was why I would help his wife take care of the aged Tobiah with dementia.

*I packed up my active little boy, who was not yet
2-years old, in the stroller my sisters bought for
him, and walked the sixteen blocks to my mother's
house several times a week during the summer. I
was not wired to be alone and I spent too many
days alone. There were people at my mother's
house. My siblings were teenagers and young
adults, my aunt and uncle lived there. Other family
and friends came in and out all day almost every
day. It was a happy house. There was always food
cooking, music playing in one room, the noise of the
television in another, and my son loved playing in
the yard.*

*As soon as Tobiah left in the morning for
whatever it was he left home to do, I packed up to
leave for the day. As long as I made it back before
dark, it would be okay. Tobiah used the daylight
time well. It didn't get dark in Chicago until almost
9 pm and he was usually out until a little after 10
pm every day. I am not certain what he did. I had
no intention of attempting to find out. I loved the
peace and quiet. Wasn't a wife supposed to miss
her husband while he was away? Wasn't she
supposed to be happy when he came in the door
every evening?*

*The walk did me well, Nehemiah loved it too. He
was intrigued by the cars speeding by and seemed
to be delighted by the sounds of the outside. We
passed a small playground in the park on the way.*

No way could I walk past the swings and slide without giving him a chance to wet his whistle. He did not need to stay long, just a bit. A few slides down the sliding board and at least ten minutes on the swing was enough. He would allow me to put him back in the stroller to finish our journey. It was the day I decided not to stop that he objected with his crying.

"Hey pretty lady," I recognized the male voice and I was angry with myself because I felt a pleasing flutter in my stomach.

"PL", shouted Zack.

The flutter turned to fear of Tobiah following me. He had followed me before. Drip. I saw him hiding behind the cars, the trees, and on the steps of some of the houses behind me as I walked. Drip. Drip. I never stopped to acknowledge his presence, I felt he needed to follow me to feel at ease. So, I just kept walking as if I didn't see him. Drip.

"Paula, it's me, Zack."

This time I seemed to turn involuntarily. I quickly locked eyes with him and I couldn't stop the big smile quickly growing on my face and the warm feelings flooding my stomach.

"Zack!" I proclaimed softly, as I checked my big smile in case Tobiah was watching me from behind a tree. "How you doing? It's been a while."

"Pretty lady. You are still a beautiful princess. I thought that was you," he said with a smile. "It's good bumping into you. That smile of yours is still gorgeous."

"Flattery might get you everywhere," the words just slid off my tongue. Zack was always so easy to talk to. That is what me and Tobiah didn't have. We didn't just talk, we weren't friends.

"Hey Sunshine!"

"I'm on my way to my mom's house. I'm stopping in the park though, pull into the parking lot," I pointed south, "it's right up the street on the next block."

Instead Zack parked on the street, got out of his car, and walked with us.

"Who's this big guy?", he asked, while reaching out his hand to Nehemiah. "Hey Lil Man. I'm uncle Zack. How ya doin?"

"This is Nehemiah, he just turned two this month," I interjected.

We began to talk as if the last time we spoke was two years ago. Zack wanted to explore the world and sow his oats as they say. But I found God, I discovered who the negro was, I discovered my heritage and I wanted to explore that. God had my ear, I easily gave my ear to Tobiah, and Zack had no ear for it at all. Zack had enlisted in the Air Force a few months after graduation and headed out to California. Once he left, we simply lost contact. Nobody had cell phones or social media back then so losing contact with family and friends was pretty easy. We did not spend much time together that summer because I was driven to Bible class and Zack was driven to have fun.

Nehemiah had fun that day, he got to stay in the park a lot longer than usual. Zack and I took turns pushing Nehemiah on the swing and catching him on the slide. He even helped him make shapes in the sand. Nehemiah, Zack, and I were happy for a few hours as we played together like children. We sat on the park bench where I could easily keep my eye on Nehemiah playing. Neither one of us looked at each other. Both of us kept our eyes on Nehemiah.

"Man in the Mirror" by Michael Jackson played on the radio owned by the young boy on a bike.

"This song is about a man who attempts to make himself a better man before trying to change the world," I started.

"...and I also think he's relaying situations in his life that have really affected him," added Zack.

"...it sounds as if he is giving sound advice."

"...yeah, he advises the listener to reconsider his or her life and commit to taking the necessary actions to change."

"...he sees the starving children and he realizes how he never paid attention before," I offered.

"...I don't think he COULD pay attention to it before he took a good look at his own deficiencies and faults."

"...he thought of himself because he could never see the suffering of others."

"...he could see the homeless man and the woman pretending she is not lonesome...Mike's reference to children not having enough food in their belly's is a juxtaposition of his own wealth. He's making reference to the differences in the poor and people who are well off," Zack noticed.

"...his questions about him being blind can be both a metaphor for a person who is actually physically blind or him posing a rhetorical question because we know people see what they want to see."

"...he realized he was being selfish not to consider the needs of others while he lived well...can you see the imagery in, 'a summer's disregard, a broken bottle top,'" asked Zack?

"...yeah, I see a man's inner soul, a carefree summer, loneliness, and depression."

"...a broken heart and his reference to dreams deferred, images of physical scars, hurt and abuse follows the pattern of the wind."

"...he's acknowledging that he is now able to see that there are people around him living and existing with broken hearts," I confessed.

"...and reminds the listener that we have to stop it ourselves, we have to make changes within ourselves. This is when things around us will change," he hinted.

It wasn't a debate or an argument. It was a simple discussion, not complicated. We simply added to one another's thoughts and finished one another's sentences. But I had a real conversation with somebody who cared what I thought, with someone who knew that I COULD think, with someone who cared to hear what I thought.

"Would you rather slide down a rainbow or jump from cloud to cloud?", he started.

"Would you rather have wings but can't fly or gills and can't swim?", I continued with a chuckle.

"Would you rather have a pet dinosaur or a pet dragon?", Zack answered back with a "gotcha".

"Would you rather only be able to whisper or have a very loud voice?", I added with a giggle.

"Would you rather meet a superhero or a cartoon character?", he laughed with his chest puffed out.

"Would you rather live under the ocean or on mars?", I laughed back.

"Would you rather drink sour milk or eat rotten eggs?", he gave a joyous whoop and fist pump!

"Ugh! You won, that's nasty." We both laughed really hard.

I enjoyed that laugh. I missed talking to my friend. I missed having intelligent conversations with any friend, since I allowed Tobiah to isolate me from all my friends. He tried to isolate me from my family too, but they wouldn't stop coming around or calling and I wouldn't stop walking to my family's home in the warm months. He suggested I only needed him, family and friends were not important. I agreed, but in this connotation, it seemed kind of unusual and even sick.

"I love Michael Jackson's Bad album. Do you have it at home? It seems like you love it too," said Zack.

"No, I'm not allowed to listen to worldly music at home," I replied.

*"Hmmmm okay," is all Zack responded. His
response wasn't judgmental. We stumbled into a
conversation about happiness.*

"Are you happy?", I asked.

*"I try. What is happening inside us is what makes
us happy. We can't allow what is happening
around us to make us happy, we cannot allow life's
challenges to determine our happiness," said Zack.*

*"Yeah, you're right. We cannot depend on others
to make us happy," I replied.*

*"Happiness comes from within, from what is going
on inside us between our ears, the things we think
about, and the person we are," Zack added.*

*"The things we allow God to grow in us, this is
where happiness comes from," I laughed.*

*Tobiah rarely just talked to me like I am a
human, like I am a woman or a friend. Drip. His
conversations were always preachy. He was always
trying to teach me and make me a righteous person.
When that was not his job. I am the only one who
can make me righteous. He claims my salvation is
not personal.*

*"It's my job as husband to teach you," Tobiah
always said. Drip.*

"But my salvation is personal," I thought. If I have to go before the throne of judgement, I will have to account for my own actions, for the things I did. Tobiah cannot save me. He needs to figure out how to save himself and be more confident so he can stop judging me and accusing me. Having a simple conversation and being treated like a human being felt good. Drip.

"Who is Lil Man's daddy?"

"His name is Tobiah, a brother I met at Bible class. Nehemiah looks just like his daddy's daddy..."

"Is, what's his name again?"

"Tobiah," acknowledging his question.

"Is, To-bi-ah," Zack repeated slowly. Is Tobiah kind to you?"

"Why do you ask?"

"I sense something."

"What do you sense?", I was flattered my old friend was concerned.

"I sense that you have lost your sunshine," he revealed.

Silence. Silence. More silence. Drip.

"What time you got?" I asked

"It's a little after two."

"After lunch? Nehemiah missed his lunch. I'm surprised he's not fussy. He missed his nap too. I need to be on my way."

I rushed to get Nehemiah snug in his stroller. Tobiah has probably been blowing up mama's phone looking for me. I try too hard to try to keep him temperate and now how do I explain where I've been all morning? Drip.

"Let me take you Lil Man the rest of the way," offered Zack.

"No, I want to finish my walk," I lied. I did want the ride, but I could not chance Tobiah seeing me get out of Zack's car. I guessed he may be there waiting for me since he couldn't reach me on mom's phone. He was constantly checking on me. Suddenly I felt like his prisoner. A stupid prisoner. Drip.

"No, I want to finish my walk," I repeated. "It will give Nehemiah a chance to get in a nap before my family is all over him."

I reached in the diaper bag for Nehemiah's snack bag, then gave Zack a big hug. He hugged me tightly and kissed me gently on the cheek. I forgot to look around to watch for Tobiah. I was always watching, but for these few hours I forgot.

"I will be at the house on Winchester for my six-week leave then they stationing me overseas. You can reach me there. Here is the number."

He handed me a small piece of paper I knew I wouldn't keep. I slipped it into the diaper bag, temporarily until I could commit it to memory.

"Don't let him steal your sunshine PL, you don't owe anyone," he advised.

"It was good seeing you Zack, I better go now, my mother has the same phone number and address. Leave me a message there," I responded. "I like our friendship; I love how it feels."

Zack simply responded with a smile.

"Be strong and find what feels right. You found religion and it seems you found a different kind of culture," he added as his eyes admired my garment.

It was the first time in our brief encounter Zack acted as if he recognized my new look. It was a dress I made for myself, lilac and cream cotton with splashes of pastel pink in a kente type pattern, sheer cream short sleeves and thin fringes made into the fabric resemble a Native American style, but with a slim chord of blue, with a thin belt around my waist.

Tobiah said he liked the dress because he thought the belt looked like a chastity belt.

A chastity belt? I should have known then Tobiah had an archaic mindset. He would have fit in comfortably with the King Henry VIII, the king who killed his wives at his whim. If he could, he would have me in a chastity belt, used as an anti-temptation device during the Crusades. It would be just the thing he thought he needed to keep me from giving myself to any man who crossed my path. It would be perfect to dissuade me from all the sexual partners and sexual temptations he thought I couldn't keep myself from.

Since Tobiah put himself in charge of my salvation, instead of on his own, it seemed only usual that he would think an unusual thought like the belt on my comfortable summer dress was a tortuous, annoying, and primitive chastity belt, which had nothing to do with The God of Israel and the culture He described in His Word. The chastity belt was created by old evil European men to cause anguish to and control women who could so very easily control themselves merely because they wanted to do the right thing.

The dress had a very thin cord of blue with a matching headwrap and matching earrings. I grew up watching my mother and her sisters put fringes on curtains they hung on our windows. I refused to be lazy and use those same types of fringes on my clothes. I would not humiliate myself looking like my mother's drapes. While I was at home alone so often, I taught myself how to make earrings using cardboard, wire, and fabric.

"I love the wrap too," Zack said, attempting to hold on longer.

I smiled again. I walked away first, headed to my family's home, where I felt safe and secure.

"I treat you better than any other man would," explained Tobiah.

I believed it at first, but after studying couples who appeared happy and watching sisters who smiled all the time, I refused to believe that anymore. What was wrong with me? Why couldn't I be loved? Why couldn't I be treated with due benevolence? The brothers claimed that meant all the sex one wanted, but no, it meant simple human kindness. It was as if I was walking on eggshells. I wondered when the fear began. I noticed the drip a few weeks before our "marriage", but I didn't want to make a big deal of it. I made light of it. I discounted my feelings.

"What is so interesting about your spouse?"

It was the question on the table as we talked with two other young couples sitting at our table. Each couple took their turn responding to the conversation question. I listened to the compliments and the exhortations the couples gave to one another. They were heartwarming and brought tears to my eyes.

Tobiah, "I don't know the meaning of the word interesting." Drip.

Then, he laughed as he pulled me in for a side hug. Drip.

"I was just joking sweetie pie," he laughed. Drip. Drip.

"I have a joke," announced Tobiah. "A married couple is lying in bed together sleeping when the phone rings. It is 2 am. The husband answers the phone and, after a second or two replies, 'How am I supposed to know? We're 40 blocks off the lakefront!' and hangs up. The wife rolls over and asks, 'Sweetheart, who was that?' 'I don't know,' said the husband. 'It was some unsuspecting bastard asking if the coast is clear.' Isn't that hilarious?"

Drip and Drip.

If I said something about the abuse disguised as a joke in front of other people, Tobiah would likely either give me a hug and say he didn't mean it or look at me like I'm crazy because of my reaction. This happened quite a bit in our years together. Drip. My premise is that Tobiah needed to make *sure other people believed I was overly emotional so his stories and lies about me stuck. Not long after, Tobiah began to call me stupid.*

The feast of Tabernacles 1980 was the first time Tobiah made an insulting joke about me in public. It was common for him to make insulting jokes or put me down when we were alone. He ridiculed my abilities, my personality, my heritage, my family, my education, my cooking, my sewing, my housekeeping. It grew to everything I did or created or said. But it wasn't all the time. The ridicule came in spurts. If I told him I was hurt, he told me I was too sensitive. The drip was getting annoying, but you don't sell your house over a leaky faucet, right? When a playful joke was a little more than playful, I told myself he didn't really mean it. Drip.

By the time we got home, the accuser left, and my loving husband was home with me alone. I longed for those moments when he was gentle and kind and loving and complementary. He catered to me that night and made love to me gently. I was drawn in again.

He used to call me sunshine
said I brightened up his day
said I gladdened his moment
that's what he used to say

He used to smile when I walked up
said I brightened up his day
said I made him feel at ease
that's what he used to say

His friendship never gated me
said I brightened up his day
said I was a special thing
that's what he used to say

Tobiah took a second job that summer, he was
never afraid of work. He worked first shift, so he
wasn't off until 3 in the afternoon. On the days I
walked to my family's home, he picked me up by
3:30. Tobiah wasn't as astute as he thought; he
never even suspected. Zack and I met at the park
several times before he was deployed. Our visits
were always in public; between brunch until mid-
afternoon, with Nehemiah present. We watched him
play.
I had so much fun during these simple visits. I
made lunch for us some afternoons. Other times he
brought lunch for all three of us. Zack was my
friend. I loved our impromptu visits, our mere

conversations; our clean, crimeless, inculpable chats. We read "Kindred" by Octavia Butler together that summer. It was a novel which incorporates time travel and intermingles science fiction with a familial slave narrative. It made for engaging conversation, as we talked about our favorite characters. It drew us into conversations about race, marriage, survival, and the dark history of America.

Zack and I never touched outside of a hello or goodbye hug. He never tried to kiss me; he was always respectable, and I made sure I stayed my physical distance. I don't know what Zack was thinking, but I never had any impure thoughts about being physical. I had to prove to myself that I was not a whore and I had no desire to throw myself on any man. It was good having a friend to talk to and listen; someone to treat me with kindness with whom I could just be myself.

Zack told me about a young lady named Faith he met in San Diego that he didn't want to fall in love with. He talked to her on the phone a lot while he was in Chicago. He wished she was his best friend. I encouraged him that it would be as easy to be her best friend as it was to be mine, all he had to do was allow himself to love. My visits with Zack made me feel good about myself. He gave me courage and I encouraged him to open his heart to love. It was a good summer. When I said goodbye to Zack at that first week in, he had no idea I had made up my mind to leave Tobiah and go back to my family home.

My mother knew what I was dealing with when I left home to be with Tobiah after our so-called wedding, with neither his family nor mine to witness and celebrate. She tried to warn me.

"My dear sweet girl, this man will throw you away like a dirty dish rag when he is done with you."

"No, he won't mama, Tobiah is not like that; he is a man of God," I defended him.

"What kind of man of God will take a beautiful and intelligent young woman away from her family and pretend to be married," she asked through her tears.

"Mama, we don't need the White man's piece of paper to prove our love for one another. We said vows to The Most High and God takes it very seriously. We have a marriage covenant we respect," I said quietly.

"Don't do this," mama pleaded. "It's a mistake."

"Mama, you gotta let me go and be my own woman," I said stupidly.

That was the conversation my mother and I had in the beginning, when she should have smacked the taste out of my mouth. Now, I have a son to consider. Tobiah already told me he could not be Nehemiah's father if I left him. I didn't believe him, I thought it was just another ploy to be in control and to keep me from leaving. In the past, if Tobiah suspected I was at wits end and ready to leave, he laid on the charm. He would do things like bring me flowers or candy. He would surprise me with a night out, just the two of us. Once he even whisked me away on a romantic stay at a downtown hotel since we didn't have a honeymoon. During those times he'd be sweet and kind, and I'd fall in love all over again, forgetting about my thoughts of leaving. He modified his behavior just long enough for me to believe he had truly changed.

However, this time, I missed my summer rendezvous with Zack. It wasn't that I missed Zack, I just missed having someone to talk to. I missed feeling valued and I missed feeling I was important with something important to say. I missed that Zack was not there to listen to me, nobody could ball and chain Zack. Tobiah's charm was temporary and I was tired of feeling like I was swinging on a yo-yo. I realized my value and I was tired of allowing Tobiah to fill in the blank spaces with his contradictory constructs.

So, one night, I told my mother I was not going back. Yet, I feared Tobiah enough to leave him with no information and no reasons why. I did not want to get back on that emotional yo-yo and ride until I was strong enough. As if she had been waiting for this revelation, she immediately called my uncle in Michigan City and told him to drive up in the *morning to pick me up. He didn't hesitate since he drove from Michigan City to Chicago almost every weekend. My mother knew I needed to hide myself if I was to stay away long enough to wean myself of Tobiah's charm.*

I spent the fall season that year in Michigan City with Uncle and Auntie hiding, so I could think and draw close to God for myself. Tobiah was my head, my covering, but in covering me, his covering sprued venom through my soul; a venom for which I had no antidote. I wrote him several letters with no return address and sent pictures of Nehemiah for him to enjoy his growth. I talked to Nehemiah about his Abah and had a picture of him next to Nehemiah's bed so he wouldn't forget his face.

While there I made sure I read my Bible. I read it more that fall in Michigan City than I had at home with Tobiah. I seemed drawn to it now whereas, at home I was drawn to walk those eggshells carefully trying to prevent outbursts and rages. My focus was on the red writing in the New Testament, I wanted to know what the Messiah said about things. I also read about the lives of women and how they related to and were guided by their husbands. Abraham listened to Sarah. Isaac listened to Rebbeccah. And though Jacob had no love for Leah, he did not abuse her. Her torment was caused by her jealousy for the love he had for her sister. I wondered what would happen if Leah would have refused to take her sister's husband. I doubt if her father would have killed her, what else could he have done? Would it have been worse than the torment of being unloved? I knew what being a rejected wife felt like, what could be worse?

I read the story of Samuel's mother, her husband listened to her and comforted her. Boaz was concerned about rumors that would surface if someone in the community saw Ruth leaving his presence early in the morning. He did not start the rumors, he dispelled them. Even Queen Esther was able to get the king's ear to save her people. The men in the community listened to Huldah tell them what the scriptures they found meant and how to respond to what they read. Neither her husband nor the men in the community talked down to her, they listened to what she had to say. Deborah even led Israel in battle, and Barak would not go unless she did because he knew she was the one anointed by The Father. Her husband Lapidoth did nothing to stop her.

There were women in the scriptures who were treated with respect. Moses allowed a bill of divorcement because hard hearted Israelite men mistreated their wives. The Messiah said that too. I discovered Ephesians 5 where it said, "Submitting yourselves one to another in the fear of God, THEN "wives, submit yourselves unto your own husbands, as unto the Lord." I had no problem submitting to my husband. I wanted him to be the head, I was not trying to wear the pants in the family, but when was he going to submit to me? All I wanted Tobiah to do was trust me, love me and stop accusing me of giving myself to other men. I needed someone who practiced the fruit of the spirit and encouraged me to grow in them. Tobiah had it twisted, and I needed

151

to learn to love him from a distance. Placing myself on the outside looking in, I could see more clearly.

I stayed there the rest of August and all of September. Uncle got me a part time job at a tutoring agency, the owner was a retired educator and attended his church. I had four steady clients, a few blocks away. He had been a teacher in the Michigan City school system for 40 years and the agency was his retirement project. It was only open Monday through Thursday from 3:30 - 7:00 pm. He had twelve school aged children and six high school students who were still struggling in basic skills. I found out at the agency that I had a natural ability to teach. I planned to go to college to become an educator. He had two other tutors, besides me. One was his nephew, Wayne Banks.

It seemed Wayne was a local celebrity. He sang in my family's church choir on Sunday, or should I say he blew the place up with his voice. I attended church on a few Sundays with Uncle and Auntie every now and then. Their church had a really energetic praise and worship team. It's too bad the Israelites I know couldn't get with it. I never understood why because the Bible study seems to be for us, but the praise and worship is in accordance to the Word of God. I read in the book of Psalms, "Praise ye the Lord. Sing unto the Lord a new song, and his praise in the congregation of saints. Let Israel rejoice in him that made him: let the children of Zion be joyful in their King. Let them praise his name in the dance: let them sing praises unto him with the timbrel and harp." This was enough for me to know we should be praising God as passionately as we teach His Word.

Sometimes life puts you on a path and won't let you off. Wayne taught me that our paths are controlled by our choices. The energy we put into making these choices is what puts us on these paths. So, then, it is not life who puts us on a path, it's me, you, he and she. We do it to ourselves. Wayne was a path I should not have chosen.

He sang at the local bar several nights a week. He was good at drawing people in. His charm and charisma made people want to listen to him and follow him. And to top it off he was fine. He was a good looking, Black man with beautiful dark chocolate skin as smooth as butter; standing tall, about 6 feet 3 inches and more self-confident than Sidney Poitier. Wayne was, in fact, too self-confident; he was arrogant and cocky. He was a sexual predator and it was common knowledge his history was to groom young women he deemed vulnerable and train them to be his secret sex pets, but nobody told me. It's a good thing he wasn't a minister. He'd misled tons of folks and had no remorse about it. And his bull's-eye was me.

I think Wayne was skilled in giving girls mad butterflies. He put a huge smile on my face when he looked at me. It was crazy how much I liked him. The old women would say, "he made my head swim." I forgot about right and wrong. I forgot about my strong desire to be a wife and be loved, instead of looked upon with disdain. I forgot to keep my panties pulled up and my dress pulled down. Some nights I'd fall asleep talking to him on the phone and wake up a few hours later and he'd still be on the phone. I wished I had a marriage license so I could tell him I was married.

Wayne took me to the club to listen to him sing on a Friday night. I knew the Shabbat was beginning, but my plan was to simply listen and not buy anything. I was fooling myself. After the set I went to his dressing room, so I wouldn't feel like I was in the club on the sabbath. He had another set to go and I thought I'd wait it out in there. He was easy to talk to, as easy as Zack. He didn't mind me talking to other guys while he was in the room. We didn't look at it as a threat, he seemed to trust me. He'd simply come over and hold my hand or put his arm around my shoulders. He moved with a crew of other young cocky guys and their girls. He wasn't intimidated by my intelligence and liked it when I dressed up; Tobiah preferred I dress down.

Wayne never missed it when I did my hair differently, he always noticed and loved it. He was not overly protective. Wayne was much more charming than Tobiah, full of compliments. He called me "Pretty Lady" each time he greeted me. It felt good. After the final set that Friday night, the time I knew I should be at home reading Bible stories to Nehemiah, Wayne insisted I go with him to an after set at one of his guy's houses. I went with no resistance.

Twenty minutes into our arrival, Wayne was on the other side of the room giving all his attention to another young lady. Then, her young man was on the couch sitting a little too close to me making small talk. The host of the house brought out joints in a small bowl and pills on a small platter, for what he called, "everyone's enjoyment". I noticed Wayne rejected the bowl of joints and opted for the platter of pills instead. He then pulled out a small white plastic bag half full of a white powder from his jacket pocket. He made two small rows of the powder on the table in front of the love seat where he and the other girl sat, and they had at it before they began to kiss. My mouth hung wide open.

I looked over at the guy sitting next to me, he had told me his name, but I didn't really hear it. When I looked at him to see if he saw his girlfriend and my boyfriend kissing, he asked me did I prefer a joint, pills, or what Wayne had. Then, he leaned in and tried to kiss me. The host and a girl, who was not his girlfriend, were busy in the large chair on the other side of the room and another couple made their way to the bedroom.

I felt as if there was a spirit in my left ear saying, "Go ahead, don't be a prude, kiss him; a pill will get you there faster than a joint". In my right ear, I heard "Therefore to him that knoweth to do good, and doeth it not, to him it is sin". I got up and left. I walked as far as I could and stopped at the gas station to call Uncle to pick me up. He asked questions on the way to his house that I avoided.

When Wayne called later that night I didn't answer. I didn't answer when he called the next day or the day after that either. I ignored him at the tutoring agency on Monday. Tobiah was not good for me, but as I thought of Wayne, I knew I could not fix a disaster by creating a catastrophe. I wasn't sure if I had committed adultery or fornication and there are not levels to sin in God's mind. What is it called when boyfriends swap girlfriends? I know when couples are married, it's called wife swapping. It was too much for me to comprehend. Call me old fashioned but I like a man who would not trade me with his friend at his whim. I was not going to be turned into a harlot nor a drug addict! No way!

"Father forgive me for being weak for companionship," I prayed deeply that night. "I'm sorry, Father, against you only have I sinned. Please accept my sincere repentance. I will try to do better and be better." I pleaded. "I got myself in this mess and I need you to help get me out of it."

I'm Sorry

I am so sorry, Lord Adam, please forgive me for
    getting us into this mess
I should'da listened to you, I should'da walked
    away when I heard it wasn't your voice
I should'da told you when that serpent first spoke to me
How can I ever be trusted again?
I am so sorry please forgive me Lord.

I promise to help you all I can
I promise to do my part while you work to till the
ground by the sweat of thy face

156

I promise you Adam, you are not alone
I'm here to help you till these thorns and thistles
The herbs of this field are not as pleasant as those
we ate in the garden.

But I promise I will do everything
I can to make them pleasant to your taste and
pleasing to your palate
This tent our new home is not as pretty as the
garden and
It doesn't smell as good
But I promise I will do everything I know how to
make you comfortable in it.

I'm here Adam, I promise to help you all I can
The Lord said my desire would be to you, my
husband
He said my sorrow and my conception would be
greatly multiplied
He said I would bring forth your children in sorrow
and great pain
I will try to be a good mother to your seed and our
children
I will try to help you teach them in the way they
should go.

You are to rule me my husband
I hope you can find it in your heart to have mercy
on me
I hope you can rule me with kindness because of
what I have done.

You are my head, my desire is to you my lord

Oh my God..., These curses are too deep for me
I can hardly bare it Lord what will happen to us?
What will happen to our children?
Oh Yahuah, Jesus, Jehovah, Yahweh, God I'm sorry
I should'da listened to Adam's instruction. Please
* forgive me.*

I was thinking of enrolling the Community
College, but it would be too difficult in Michigan
City. I didn't have a car, the buses didn't run as
well as in Chicago, and my mother and sisters were
my support system. I needed help with Nehemiah if
I was going back to school. I had to find direction
for my life if I was going to be single again and
raise my son. I also did not want to keep Nehemiah
away from his father too long. A boy needs his
father. I had been away long enough to be strong
enough to know that I did not have to be Tobiah's
wife any longer, but he would always be
Nehemiah's father and he needed to know where
Nehemiah was so he could pick him up for visits.
Since we had no lawful marriage license, this was
an easy out of an uneasy situation.

I felt free to make decisions and draw close to
God on my own. I also needed to get back to
Chicago as my family prepared for the holidays.
They made a big thing out of Halloween,

Thanksgiving, Christmas, and New Year's and I didn't want Nehemiah around it. They had small children and they wanted their children to have a good time during this season. I didn't want to confuse him, and I didn't want to offend my uncle and his family because they had been very good to me us while we were there.

Nehemiah would be safer in Chicago because my mother was not that into the holidays. Her celebrations took place at her church, she didn't decorate or anything so Nehemiah couldn't learn to admire the festivities. My sisters were young women living the life of a young woman of the world, but they didn't care much about decorations and holiday parties, they just wanted to be pretty and fly, be cool, and be amazing to their other young friends. But they loved Nehemiah, and didn't mind babysitting at least sometimes, all I needed was their sometimes.

I needed to get away from Wayne, he was not good for me either. So, I decided to leave my uncle's hospitality a week before Halloween, when the decorations would be put up. I arranged for my father to drive to Michigan City, since he lived in Benton Harbor, and drive me back to Chicago. He asked me why I didn't come to Benton Harbor, and I appreciated the offer, but I knew I would have the same problems there since he was a musician and he was on the road a lot.

I wouldn't have a support system to take classes in somebody's college and I would need a car. CTA and Metra were plentiful and easy in Chicago. Nehemiah would be three soon and I needed to figure out what to do with my life. My sisters could rotate caring for him while I was in class. And Chicago State University was only 5 blocks away, I could walk.

I seemed like a good plan. I had no thoughts of running into Tobiah; I was past his charm. It was September 23rd and I had a plan. My father would pick me up October 25th. I had one month to work my plan. I sent for the admissions papers to Chicago State so I could be in class in January. The admissions packet arrived in only 3 days and I would have it completed and mailed back the same day. The school would have it back before I arrived.

"Thank you for giving me another chance," he gently whispered in that charming voice that took away my mental and emotional strength. "I promise I will do right by you," he whispered.

"You promise Tobiah?", I countered with more confidence than I had before.

"I took you for granted and I apologize, please forgive me," he appealed.

We were back to the usual pre-Michigan City escapades in less than a month. Before I knew it, I was in the midst of the cycle of abuse again. The honeymoon was over, and I was being accused of sleeping with every man who crossed my path again. It wasn't better after I told Tobiah I was nine weeks pregnant. It wasn't worse either. It was the same as before. I wrote Wayne a letter telling him about the baby, but he never responded, and I was glad. My admissions application was accepted, but I never stepped foot in a classroom. Over the years I learned Tobiah could control the evil spirit that inhabited him for up to six months. I learned to enjoy his charm and his love three to six months at a time.

Tobiah never mentioned Wayne. He accepted my pregnancy and took care of Wayne's daughter like she was his own. I appreciated him for that, and his attempt to forgive kept me with him for so long.

"I know we don't need man's piece of paper to make us married, we made a covenant with one another, but it didn't quite feel like I was married. Maybe if we had it, I wouldn't have made that awful mistake with Wayne."

I persuaded Tobiah and we got that marriage license, but our families still weren't there. We went to city hall. It was a compromise for a wedding and loving witnesses.

"Emah, why you sad all the time? You don't like me? You don't like to watch me play in the park no more," Nehemiah asked inquisitively.

"I love you Nehemiah. You are a gift to me from God. I love to watch you play," I comforted my young son.

I didn't realize I was frowning so much, and I certainly did not want my unhappiness to affect my babies at all. So, from that day forward I plastered a smile on my face. I stood in the mirror and used my fingers to put the corners of my mouth in position to smile. Once I saw the smile, I wanted my babies to see, I closed my eyes to feel the smile. I wanted to be able to show my children that smile without looking in the mirror. My children deserved a smile.

Every morning when I opened my eyes, I didn't want to raise my head from the bed until I felt a smile on my face. I lay there awhile as I listened to Tobiah prepare himself for his workday, hoping the children wouldn't wake from the noise. I laid there with my eyes closed to talk to myself so I could make it through just one more day. Inside my head, I also sang and prayed. Some days I didn't want to breathe anymore but my children kept me going. They were given to me to nurture and to love. The

Most High helped me, He heard my cries and one day I couldn't cry anymore. My tears dried up and before I knew it, I didn't have to plaster a smile on my face anymore. It was through Christ that I found myself strengthened.

Tobiah had names ready for the boys, but he didn't have one ready for Salachyah. I didn't hold it against him. I understood. I was not in a position to push. I wondered if I had another girl if he would want to name her. My baby girl was no mistake. She brought so much joy to my heart. The Most High sent her to me as he sent King David his son Solomon after his chastisement. Salachyah would grow to do great things too because I was going to nurture her with prayer and love.

The man who dropped off the diapers for diaper service. The man sitting at the light waiting for it to change. The brother who volunteered to teach martial arts to the boys at the church. The brother hired to teach math at the school where I worked. The stranger walking past me in the store. The owner of the stance studio where I took Zumba. The brother who cut the neighbor's grass. The cashier at the grocery store. Or any other man with whom I accidently made eye contact. The accusations were continuous. It was always

unexpected, and it was still utterly ridiculous and extremely hurtful.

If I cried or acted like my feelings were hurt, I knew I needed to be ready for the ridicule like it was my fault he hurt me with his tongue. As if I caused it because I was too sensitive anyway. According to Tobiah, I didn't have anything to be upset about.

"You aren't even good for a good fight," I heard often as I tucked myself in the corner chair to cry.

There were many days I allowed the demon to steal my joy. My sunshine was very sparing. Like a yo-yo, his temperament would be the exact opposite. He was gentle, used kind words, and even looked at me as if I was beautiful in his eyes. He spoke of my goodness and what a peaceful spirit I had. Sometimes he loved me, and I knew it and felt it; and other times he had a disdain for me I found too difficult to bear. I was riding a roller coaster. Yet, I loved the good in him. I began journaling to help me deal with my feelings. The constant drip of that damn faucet was not going to damage my children.

Why I Write

I write because I
hear what the voice of many waters' sings
get weary of turbulence in this life
praise Jesus the Holy King
cry because I am hurt
love to laugh instead of weep
am thankful he brought me from the dirt
wait in haste but desire to trust
pursue patience, virtue and knowledge
am being trained to shy from carnal lust
need my maker to purge sin he sees
want to be healed of the old wound and scar
thirst to deliberately stir emotion in others
love to teach young minds and shake them ajar

I write because I
feel music swirling deep in my bones
can hear the praise song in my head ring
am quickened by the rhythm in the sound
help proclaim the nobility of my people
propagate, enlighten, diversify, and expound
am part of a glorious people's past
feel the hurt and harm piercing from the bondage
want this knowledge to help our future last
pray for tender mercy, loving kindness, and the seal
love to praise and pray to The Most High
need to solidify my own inner beauty and zeal

need to reaffirm my inner strength with speed
desire to dwell in the house of God
aspire to always trust His lead
want to thank Him for allowing me to see
need to increase my faith in my Lord
seek a greater joy than man has given me

I write because I
hear the music and the song in my pen
suddenly have a whole lot to say
consistently fall and make crazy mistakes
want to leave a legacy for my precious young
understand that salvation sits on high stakes
am aware of spiritual wickedness in high places
study the cause of powers and principalities
love to put smiles on stressed out faces
have a story to tell
have a mission to reach
needed to come out of pity's shell

I write because I
flutter as I feel the cadence beat
feel a joyous pulsating trance
love the sound to jump me out of my seat
find understanding, strength, and power in my pen
seek to comfort my sentimental spirit
need a love that seems far beyond men
have done everything I can think of to do
won't give up but don't dare fall
hold on to what I know is true
lift His name on high everyday
am glad I know Jesus and the plan
am grateful for all blessings and the narrow way

Railing and Reviling

Reviling is to scold as scold is to taunt
Taunt is to chide as chide is to criticize.
Criticize is to rail as rail is to find fault with.
Find fault with is to beat down as beat down is
to terrorize.
Terrorize is to judge as judge is to intimidate.
Intimidate is as a slap in the face
A slap in the face is as malign.

Unrighteous as thieves and liars.
Sinful as adultery and drunkenness.
Wicked as idolatry and the effeminate.
Intolerable as Sabbath breaking and the slothful.
Unjust as extortion and those who covet.
Hated as the talebearer and discord sewn.
Despised as innocent blood shed.

Intimidate is to despise as despise is to hate.
Hate is to castigate as castigate is to curse.
Curse is to threaten as threaten is to unkind
language.
Unkind language is to condemnation as
condemnation is to attack.
Attack is to mistreat as mistreat is to berate.
Berate is to abuse as abuse is to accuse.
Accuse is to murder as murder is to crime.

Seeds of pride and envy.
Fruit of wrath and strife.
Purposed from envious and pernicious.
Meant to defame and beat down.
Implications of judgement and imprudence.
Not in accordance with right and justice.
Kiss New Jerusalem goodbye.

As I stood on the choir stand, just before the
music started, I spotted Zack coming in the door
with his wife, Faith, and their children. She was
obviously the one for him and at first glance, they
looked pleased with one another. Last I heard she
caused him to settle down and stop sewing his royal
oats. I was happy for him. He sent pictures of his
new babies after each birth. I waited a long time to
see him walk through that door and join me on the
road to salvation. This was a surprise. I couldn't
wait to meet his wife and give her a big hug. I was
happy to praise God that day.

"Like Jesus, I wanna please him; walk in his ways,
commandments keep them"

Mark, the brother leading the song, was not a
likeable brother. I rarely said much to him other
than, "Shalom brother Mark, how are you and your
family?" He rarely admonished anyone, especially
sisters. His communication wasn't pleasant, until

he combined it with his larynx and his diaphragm to blow the heck out of a gospel song on the Sabbath. I preferred songs that worshiped and praised Yah, and this song was more of a "teaching" song than a "praising" song, but it was most definitely one with a good melody that could make me move my feet, hands, head, shoulders and arms. And that is just what I did that day.

I closed my eyes, rolled my shoulders, bobbed my head, and grooved to the soft flow of music that permeated my whole soul that day. The choir director made a clapping motion directing us to clap, but it wasn't a clapping kind of song. It was a snap your fingers kind of melody and that is what I did. I knew my part well, so I closed my eyes for moments in the song. My feet joined in perfect sync to the beating of the heartbeat of the song. My good friends standing on either side of me in the alto section were used to my dancing on the choir stand and they moved away slightly to give me the space I needed to enjoy myself. We had an unspoken agreement.

As the song progressed, I felt relaxed, and allowed a small smile to form on my lips. My knees and shoulders moved in sync as I sang the words in prayer asking Yah to help me be like His son, whom he sent to this earth to die for my sins. It was a perfect and moving moment of praise and gratitude. Wasn't it okay to dance and sing praises to our God? Wasn't it alright to really connect with him in song and think about how much I wanted to be like Him? Wasn't it fine to praise Him because His name is excellent?

I did not want it to end, I wanted to extend it; we could have sung that song twice. I hadn't had enough. That song was da bomb and that day it was better than ever! The brothers who wrote and arranged this song moved the hell out of me. Not only the melody and arrangement moved me that day, but I was moved by the lyrics too. I loved singing in the choir. I sang alto and the alto part the choir director gave us was fire! It was my favorite part of Sabbath service. The Bible class was enlightening, and it was definitely necessary, but studying was for us. The time provided the choir to praise and worship was for The Father. It was our time to praise Him.

I made a big mistake on the choir stand that day. I should not have enjoyed the music so much. I should have thought about Tobiah and his reaction to my praise and worship, instead of focusing on The Most High God. I forgot about Tobiah. When I climbed off the choir stand and sat next to Tobiah and the children, when our eyes locked and I gave him a warm smile, he met me with a hellish stare.

"So that's your new nigga?", Tobiah snarled in his hellish mood.

I broke out in a cold sweat, paralyzed and humiliated, because the sister and her husband directly in front of us heard what he said. They looked at each other in confusion, then quickly turned their heads to the front of the church, frozen trying not to move. I knew Tobiah did not mind

170

making a scene, so nothing came out of my mouth. I felt stuck, surprised, hurt and helpless.

Turned out there was a rumor going around the church that Brother Mark was having an affair with another sister in the church. The grapevine discussed it after class, sisters were convinced it was a single sister whom Mark was attempting to add to his family. Abigail said her husband thought it was just a rumor. He did not like to add to vicious rumors. However, Tobiah had other ideas.

Before leaving, I moved through the crowd to find Zack and Faith. When I got to them, I hugged Faith first so as not to get off on the wrong foot.

"Peace and love my sister," I giggled. "I am so happy to finally meet you. My name is Paula, people around here call me Simchah."

"I am happy to meet you too, Zack told me a lot about you," Faith shrieked.

I loved her warm and lively response. I liked her a lot. I gave his children a big smile as I hugged them and introduced myself. She was happy. I knew Zack had it in him to make someone happy.

"Hey Sunshine!", he remembered.

"Zack! What are you doing here? I saw you coming in from the choir stand."

"I saw you up there jamming. You were really into that song. I was hoping we could talk before we left," interjected Zack. "We started attending the class in Houston Texas a few years ago."

"That's so exciting Zack," I am so happy for you and your family. You have got to tell me how that happened!"

"We are in Chicago for a few weeks for my father's funeral,' he responded.

"Oh, I am so sorry for your loss, when are the services?", I sighed.

"We actually had it Tuesday. We will be here for two more weeks. We need to pack up the house, I am deciding whether to put it on the market or rent it," Zack informed me. "How's the little fellow, Nehemiah? What's he up to?", he wondered.

"Nehemiah is a young man. He's away at college," I answered. "I have, wait for it, five sons and my daughter is 15. Her name is Salachyah, it means forgiveness. She brings so much joy to my life. She has the tenacious spirit I lacked most of my life. I hope to spend time with you both before you leave," I said in earnest.

Turning to look at Faith, "Do you need anything while you're here? Call me and I will help you pack up the house. Maybe we can even get a few more sisters to come help. I know moving is hell. I hate

172

it. Let me give you my number. Please feel free to call me. I know of a really nice spa in the South Loop and we can have lunch or something. It's not easy being a stranger to Chicago."

"Would you rather slide down a rainbow or jump from cloud to cloud?", I looked at Zack and said.

"Would you rather have wings but can't fly or gills and can't swim?" he continued with a chuckle.

"Would you rather only be able to whisper or have a very loud voice? Faith added with a giggle. We all cracked up.

"You know the game?", I asked Faith as we gave each other a high five.

It was a nice moment. The look on Zack and Faith's faces said thank you. They seemed relieved.

"Come, let me introduce you two to my husband, Tobiah," I beckoned to them to come to the back where Tobiah and I were sitting. But he was not there. I couldn't find him anywhere. The boys and their bags were also gone. I was embarrassed.

"We need to get out of here anyway Sunshine," Zack relieved me of the awkward moment. Faith and I gave each other another big hug and I made her promise she'd call me to come help her pack up Zack's father's things.

I had choir rehearsal and a feast committee meeting, so I did not leave right away. By the time I got home and found Salachyah with the boys, I knew I was in the center of an episode. The children were happy to see me and asked why I didn't come home with them. Tobiah left them home alone. We heard Tobiah's keys in the door a few hours later. As was the children's custom, they ran to their rooms when they heard the key scared of the mood their father would be in when he came home. They could sense his mood was not pleasant and opted to remain in their rooms to play.

I fed the children, put them to bed, and I decided to ask Tobiah what he meant by his statement to me in church. I knew what he meant but, I was afraid to stand up to him. His will was much stronger than mine and his words pierced deeper than I could think but, I had to ask this time. I just had to know why?

"You know what I meant, you got a new nigga huh?", he repeated.

"I just don't get why you keep accusing me of this heinous act. I want salvation. I want a spot in the kingdom. Why don't you know that by now?", I asked. "Why do you think this is true?" I looked him in his eyes.

To my complete and utter surprise, "I know it's true because God told me it is true," he hissed.

As usual, I abandoned my idea to stand up to Tobiah this time. Instead, I completely shut down, as usual. My heart skipped several beats. My eyes could not make contact with his eyes. My tongue felt as if it had been cut out. I could not find the words to respond because this was just not the usual accusation for which I grew accustomed. He really believed with all his heart he got these messages from Yah, The Most High. I stood there not able to move.

"If it is not true, I give up my right to the tree of life," said Tobiah believing what he said with all his heart and might.

My thoughts didn't know where to go. Who is the accuser? The word accuse means to charge with a fault or offense. I quickly reflected. I was floored. I was motionless. My feet were glued to the floor. Why in the freakin frack would a sane person even think to give up his right to the Marriage of The Lamb for a marriage built on torment and not worth the paper it's written on? The one thing I did know is that it was not God whispering in Tobiah's ear. That scared me and caused my bones to quiver under my skin.

My mind rolled back memories of all the times he accused me. "So, this is why he believed it with his whole heart," I thought. I finally understand why he would storm in the house as if he knew someone else was there. I understand why he followed me hiding behind the trees as I walked to my mother's house. This is why he talked to himself

*behind closed doors as if he were in pain. He
doesn't talk to himself. He talks to an evil spirit.
This is why the voices behind the closed door
frighten me. Because the voices are demonic. I
understood why he really believed I was having an
affair with his sister's husband. "I understand it
all", I concluded as I saw these words on the page.*

*I tried my best to love Tobiah, but he wouldn't
let me love him enough. I wanted so much to be
obedient to God and be an obedient wife. All love is
not good, and all obedience is not holy. It was in
each moment as I stood motionless and speechless,
that I mustered up enough good sense to make a
decision to remove myself and my babies from that
house. I should have done it years ago, long before
we conceived six children.*

*Was this the same voice that spoke to him when
he was told I am his wife? Then this was not a
marriage from the God I read about in the Word.
That stupid statement, the one where Tobiah gave
up his right to the tree of Life, the Son of The Most
High God, Yeshuah Ha Meshiach, Jesus Christ, the
Rock of Salvation, The Rose of Sharon, The Kings
of Kings, Lord of Lords, now that's stupid! I was
afraid not to relinquish his control over me. Who
was Tobiah really following while I was following
him? The answer to this question gave me the
strength to get the hell out of there once and for all.*

*I had to be prepared for an outpouring of love
and affection. I realized a long time ago that my
husband was a misogynist and he had the ability to
turn on the charm at the drop of a hat. This time, I
would not fall for it. Tobiah grew to be a good*

*provider and I loved him when he was Tobiah. It
was the demon I needed to leave. When I figured
out how to get out, I was out.*

Scorpion's fire

*scorpion's fire ensnares the soul
disobeys the noble heart
pouring pestilence into the ear language
discord weigh not words
can't give virtue breath
jaded monster mocks
beauty poison deceits set with skill
eat of treacherous passion
subdues softly contaminates love
subtle whoredom accused
cunning adultery cited
jokes the honest bed
love never tainted
suspicions void of wit
convinced affections shared for sport
feverish flame repeatedly spoken
throwing restraints
unwarranted criticism
treachery from youth
purged true love
causes lonely to roost
silhouettes of wicked ears who saw envy*

eyes heard strife
feelings of wrath
whispers of Satan
who is the accuser
an evil jealous spirit
causes one to mistreat
abuses your blessing
venomous saga
the secret lie
causes much anger
scorpion's fire pisses God off

Whenever you find yourself in the hands of someone who does not understand your value, purpose and destiny...you will find someone who will use and abuse you. Someone who abuses you, does not understand you. The best thing you can do is remove yourself. Let go and let The Most High deal with that individual. Again, do not allow someone's dysfunction to cause you to sin against God, destroy your peace or give you bad energy.

Finally, after 21 years of living in the fear of emotional turmoil, I mustered up enough strength and courage to remove myself and my children from the grips of the mean man. Tobiah was my cross to bear and I bore it as long as I could. But what happened? My family was happy and helpful. I praise Yah He put in their hearts to help us so much with our transition. They thought I would stop living the lifestyle in which I believed. They thought I'd attend church with them on Sunday, eat the pork I hadn't eaten in years and take part in the holiday celebrations again. When these things didn't happen, they became a bit standoffish with me again. I think they just didn't understand where I was coming from and they didn't get my pain.

Change is painful, and it is very difficult to embark on the unknown. My lifestyle was still unknown to them. But it was not completely their fear of change. I was the oldest child of my eight siblings and when I embraced the Israelite lifestyle, I set my self apart from my family more than I should have. I was the one who stopped communicating. I considered my church family more family than my blood family. I was wrong. Instead, I should have been an example to them.

I could have converted them with love. It's the love we show to one another that will push us into Yah's kingdom. The Scribes and Pharisee kept the law better than anyone, and they won't get in, because they had no love. I pushed my family away, instead of drawing them into the light of Christ. My behavior was not the salt of the world. I didn't pray for them. I didn't act like a loving elder sister for many years, and that pushed them away. I did not involve myself in the intimate parts of their lives, showing them love. I had to try my best to make sure me and my children would not fall by the wayside. I had to make sure I put our lives in the hands of The Most High. Prayer became was my fortress and praise became my weapon.

There is a thing known as domestic abuse. It comes in physical and emotional betrayals. The cycle of domestic abuse must stop. It cannot be stressed enough. Do you think The Most High intended for "and thy desire shall be to thy husband, and he shall rule over thee" to be void of love and kindness? Don't you think He intended for men to lead their households applying the Fruit of the Spirit? How long will the contrary messages be taught to our daughters and sons? When will enough be enough? How long will it rent hearts before its end comes?

Let the records show these few statistics for women between the ages of 14 and 44. Domestic violence is the leading cause of injury or death. It kills more than auto accidents, muggings, and cancer deaths combined. 88% of children who live in homes where domestic abuse occurs are violent. Approximately 8,800,000 children in the U.S. are at risk of father abandonment when daddy resents mom's strength to embark on reestablishment. Or at risk of either witnessing or suffering domestic abuse.

Almost 1/3 of seniors (adults aged 59 and over) in the U.S. report being abused by their children or grandchildren, having been beaten, cursed and often neglected for their money or belongings which they possessed. It effects everyone, regardless of age, race, ethnicity, sex, social, or economic status. It leaves devastation that modifies many young and old of us. The abuser is all about control. It is not and never was or will be about love. They are angry at themselves for feeling inadequate in some way or pain they themselves saw and experienced as they grew up. Their subconscious believes it is the way it is supposed to be. They live in denial but won't admit it; nuts and crazy, blind and can't see.

Oh, we do know when we are abused. We don't want to admit it to neither ourselves, nor especially not to anyone else. We make excuses to cover up the crime, we are ashamed; but all we seek is the love and acceptance from our abuser. Our reason is that we love them. With all their flaws and impaired ways, we truly love us some him. He sees a vulnerability in a woman, and he uses it to manipulate and control. He sweeps the victim off her feet, the fairy tale Prince Charming Dream— like it's a whirlwind romance. He either locks her down in a relationship or marries her quickly, usually within two months often with no familial witnesses, so slickly.

Then, he systematically cuts her off from her support system, either by moving away or by complaining so much with his tongue "they hog your time" or "I don't like them, and they don't like me". His goal is to detach her support and systematically cut it off gradually, until she spends less and less time with her family or his, and especially friends. This time is crucial, since this is the time when the "fun" begins.

He doesn't like the way she dresses. He doesn't like the way she wears her hair. She becomes the object of his flaring tongue. "You are so stupid". "You are too fat." Or conversely "I will love you no matter how big you get." "You are trifling, you are lazy, you are…" Just fill in the blank. Until, there is no more of the real you, remaining on this sinking ship's plank.

Your self-esteem is perfectly destroyed, then may come the physical smacking or not, maybe a more constant and severe tongue lashing Then he says, "I'm sorry, I will never do it again", which is called the "honeymoon period", or phase four if you will. Then, it starts all over again; up and down, off and on, in and out won't be still.

The average domestic abuse victim leaves their abuser seven times before they leave for good—or die—could be a spiritual or physical death. Or wait she may plot to hurt him and are successful to a dismal and deadly despair. How many will be the charm for her? She could be "merely" called every name in the book. Humiliated in public or not spoken to and ignored for six months, feeling his anger at every stare. She could be stabbed, raped, beaten, thrown down the stairs or beat down til she doesn't care.

Still she goes back. No one understands how completely defeated a victim feels if they have never been one. This is the hardest thing for a friend or family member to watch. They put their all into helping the victim get out, to help a loved one successfully leave a bad situation and then they

*don't leave or then they go back to the source of
sheer vexation.*

*Tobiah never hit me, so I was confused about my
own abuse. I talked to women who went back to
their abuser after suffering horrible injuries. One
woman got hit in the head so often she always had a
black eye and is deaf in her right ear. I talked to a
young pregnant woman whose boyfriend tied her
down, beat her in the arms and legs til they were
swollen, not wanting to hurt his unborn child. I
know women who have had broken limbs after
"falling down the stairs". Where is the honor of
man and wife? Others "only" suffer emotional
trauma, leaving she and her children debilitated for
life.*

*Deciding to leave or stay and risk being killed by
or killing someone instead is a task more difficult
than breathing. More children suffer, become
unproductive, and are at-risk—being witnesses to
abuse, than being at-risk due to poor or
husbandless parenting. You don't have just you—to
think about, what about the children? What are
their chances of being abused or even being the
abuser who mars? This situation is as dangerous
as children running in front of passing cars.*

*I see a lot of men asking for a God-fearing
woman. Then the Lord sends you one and you, in
turn, sends her away. So, The Most High sends you
another and you treat her bad. How many more do
you think he's going to send you? A King has no
intention of trying to change, control, or "shut up"
a Queen. A mentally mature man wants his woman
just as strong and tactfully outspoken as him, with*

her own mind, because he knows his woman's strength is a reflection of his own and fully understands that iron sharpens iron. A weak man, on the other hand, only approaches weak minded females, so he can be an Alpha male by default. Only in my pain. did I find my will. Only in my chaos, did I learn to be still. Only in my fear, did I find my might. Only in my darkness, did I see God's light.

These are not made up scenarios and facts, this is an undeviating domestic violence pattern. And if you recognize yourself in these statistics, there is only one thing to say...get out now. And don't go back; slowly and carefully make life new. As I live, I have come to see first-hand, some men are victims of abuse too.

My church 'family' labeled me a whore, a sinful woman, a liar, an unruly female, and a troublemaker. The men feared me because "he" said I committed adultery. The women feared me because they thought I wanted their husbands. They all feared me, because my silenced spirit made me look as if I were a rebellious and stubborn woman. Rebellion is as the sin of witchcraft, while stubbornness is as idolatry. Nobody wants such a woman around. So, I was shunned.

I could look someone in the eye and say "Shalom" and they would look at me in disdain and walk away without saying a word or uttering a sound. They refused my contributions for the feasts. Someone tried to push me off the choir stand after we sang and were dismounting. My good friends stopped calling, they stopped looking for me after Sabbath class, and they avoided me instead. If they saw me coming their way, they'd turn and walk in the opposite direction. They acted as if they were afraid of me. They never mistreated my sons, but my daughter was labeled and targeted because I was her mother. The other young girls were not allowed to play with my daughter.

I was crushed in the church I loved. They proved they were not my family. I was afraid I would be alone for the rest of my life, with no loving husband, a family I was distant from, and no real friends. So, I put my focus on making sure my children and I did not abandon God's commandments. I made sure I put my children in situations where they could gain healthy friendships. I enrolled them in baseball, softball, dancing, swimming, and other fun activities. I made sure each Sabbath we got up early and prepared ourselves to keep the day holy. I lived without the fellowship of friends and the closeness of family. I thought about living this life of fear and I realized, I was not afraid of death at all, life seemed to be a whole lot more painful than taking my long rest. I knew I was not wired to be alone but, being alone was better than being tormented.

I learned to write to release energy and gain strength. Over forty years of experiencing hurt is difficult to encapsulate, so I chronicled my pain on the pages of the journals I kept through the years as I searched for freedom and healing. Through journaling, prayer and praise, I found the power The Most High placed within me to defeat the enemy within. I have the power, because The Most High gave to me. Luke 10:19 says: "Behold, I give unto you power to tread on serpents and scorpions, and over all the power of the enemy: and nothing shall by any means hurt you."

I Got the Power

I got the power down inside myself to stand up to your put down.

It came from the same spirit that led old Noah around.

Like Noah, I can stand as you toot your mouth to scorn.

I understand the atmosphere that caused you critic to be born.

No more will I run and hide so my eyes can be filled with tears.

I've grown stronger in the Lord you see all these teary tearful years.

You critic can think what you want to think.

For I now know that it's your values and not mine that causes this awful stink.

You, critic, tried hard to lower my self-esteem.

But not even you can change the Lord's mind when he chooses me too for his team.

You have the power to alter this distorted bond. Until then, I will yearn for you to know but, there's no need to respond.

Consequently, I got the power down inside myself and I am neither angry nor afraid anymore.

The Lord Jesus in his magnificence is that firm effectual core.

In him only shall I fear

As the time of the end draws closely near.

Vengeance is not mine of course

Gotten past the heartache with much remorse.

Jesus comforts me when I am filled with sadness and sorrow.

He's shown me how to use his word for the strength I need to borrow.

His everlasting arm is bringing about healing from damages incurred.

In his word there is true restoration wisdom and counsel preferred.

His word solidifies the foundation for which loving kindness rest.

Thereby loving him I sincerely do my best.

Moreover, I got the power to be strong enough.

I got the power to be humble enough.

I got the power to be obedient enough.

I got the power to be faithful enough.

I got the power to be peaceful enough.

I got the power to be forgiving enough.

I got the power to be joyous enough.

I got the power to be patient enough.

I got the power to know enough to keep my eyes on his word, for only therein lies my power.

Zaharah walked into the room with the last journal in her hands and put out her arms to hug Simchah.

"Wow Softah, I never realized everything you went through in your life", Zaharah sighed as she held Simchah in a tight embrace. *"I stayed up all night reading your journals. I could not put them down. You are such a strong woman. Now I know why. I don't know what makes you stronger, the fact that you stayed with Saba for so long or the fact that you finally left him after so many years. And after everything he put you through, you still have enough strength to take care of Saba?"*

"My life living with a husband who could not control his demons has taught me that Elohim gives the hardest missions to His most elite soldiers. I am a soldier in this army of The Lord. My time with Tobiah didn't break me, it made me strong. I will love my neighbor as I love myself, because I love Yah and it is the right thing to do, so yes, Zaharah. I will help Joanna take care of your grandfather because it is the right thing to do." Simchah nodded as she held Zaharah. *"And Saba took care of your mother. He gave her his name. He fed her and provided for her. Though he was not a touchy feely, love 'em up kind of father, he was equally hard on her as he was all the boys, Tobiah never made a difference between his sons and Wayne's daughter. He wasn't perfect, but he had his good."*

"Grandma! What are you telling me? Are you telling me that grandpa is not really my Saba?"

Zaharah stared at Simchah in dismay and disappointment. *"Softah? I can't believe you've been acting perfect all my life, like you haven't made mistakes."*

Taking her granddaughter by the hand and looking her in the eyes, *"First of all, Zaharah, I never told you I was perfect. What makes a man or woman righteous and perfect is that when they fall, they get back up and they never make that mistake again. They may make another one, but not that one. Second, you don't get to judge me. I advise you to spend your energy getting the beam out of your own eye. How perfect are you? My last advice to you my dear is to that there is a kind of love that gives you the courage to cause you to want to be a better person and you can have that kind of love. It's the kind of love that makes you feel anything is possible. Hold out for it, you deserve it."* Zaharah nodded and smiled at her Softah's words of wisdom.

"When you fall in love, fall in love with the man who wants to know your favorite color and just how you like your tea. Fall in love with the man who loves the way you laugh and would do absolutely anything to hear it. Hold out for the man who puts his head on your chest just to hear your heartbeat. Fall in love with the man who kisses you in public and is proud to show you off to everybody they know. Wait for the man who thinks you are the most beautiful woman in a room of beautiful women and who only hears your voice among them. You

deserve the man who makes you question why you were afraid to fall in love the first place. You want the man who would never ever want to hurt you. You want the man who smiles at your flaws and thinks you are perfect in every stage of your growth. You want the man who loves to wake up to you every day. Wait and choose wisely so you won't have to learn to endure the hardship and pain from a bad marriage. There is too much other pain we must endure. Right?"

"Kan, Softah."

"Once our choices get us into hot water, we are too quick to run from the discomfort and pain of it all, from relationships that are less than ideal, because of our hastiness. Sometimes The Most High causes us to endure hardship and harshness for a higher, redemptive purpose because we refuse to hear his voice in the first place. Sometimes God's teachings are forged through hardship," Simchah sighed wiping the tears from her eyes. *"Do you hear me Zaharah?"*

"Loud and clear, Softah."

"Realize too that man will not be perfect. He will have his flaws, as do you. The Most High is witness to he and the wife of his youth. You and he will be one, that means you are a part of him, and he is a part of you so identify the beams in your own eyes and pray them out. If you are focused on the beams in your own four eyes, you will not have time to be a

busy body trying to get the mote out of the eyes of others." Simchah said lovingly, as Zaharah nodded and smiled.

"And don't idolize your husband so much that you hold him above God causing you not to communicate properly. Don't be afraid to tell him what you like and what you don't, after you talk to God about it of course. And that's it. That's my story and I am sticking to it," Simchah deeply exhaled and smiled.

"Thank you Softah for sharing your story with me, but now can we talk about the part where…" Zaharah pleaded.

"No, I don't feel like there is anything more to tell," Simchah's response was interrupted by her cell phone vibrating.

"I better answer this. Sister Joanna is probably wondering why I did not call her back last night. Let me get ready to be humble and smooth things over," Simchah said putting on her best smile.

"Good Morning Sister Joanna. Peace and love," Simchah sang, "How are you?"

Simchah's bright smile suddenly faded and turned into a look of deep concern and sadness.

"Oh, I see…I was in the middle of a project and couldn't answer the phone," she admitted, then quickly inhaled and shook her head as she closed her eyes and listened intently.

Zaharah tried to figure out what was going on, but Simchah put her finger to her lips to tell her granddaughter to be silent while she continued to listen.

"Wow, this is very unexpected. Let me get dressed and we'll be right over," Simchah sat her phone on the table as two tears streamed down her face.

"What's wrong Softah?", Zaharah asked with concern and confusion.

"Your Saba took his long rest Zaharah. He passed away in his sleep last night."

"What? No Softah!" Zaharah cried out.

"It is finished," Simchah exhaled a deep sigh of relief, because she was finally free.

12

Winds of Rose

I

This sequestered year brought with it knew light
She felt winded unnerved lonely today
People she thought she knew gave her new sight
God used "Friends" as source of new things to say
Her eyes view pity, rather than just hurt
There is a heartfelt sad deep within she
Sister Care Too Much tries always to flirt
Sister Called Hurt came by the house lately
Sister Self Pity is a willing host
Suddenly the fourth one knocks at her door
Sister Anger sneaks in long and gets close
A viral and vigorous team of four
She claims these four sisters, "they're surely mine"
Permeated sister winds over time.

II

A new sister peeped through door around ten
She vaguely recalls her spying you see
She is different from those other women
Gaining strength defines her menially
She's more like the strong aroma of myrrh
She saw other sisters sneak out the back
Sister Overcome more likely names her
They talked for a while, she's sharp as a tack

She however sees clearly who she is
Eyes shined with a clear determination
The Gospel of peace oozed out from the source,
Her feet were shod with the preparation
Couldn't have been just an overnight thing
She could hear her sing praises to the king.

III

Today was their first long talk, they would cry
Circumstances cause lives to look the same
Who is like God is the name she goes by;
Disposition more than a simple name
Polished, shined, tested, tried and now refined
Almost gave in when trials went bad to worse
Lately though her faith prayer was defined
Sister cried out when life seemed a bad curse
Mirrors the same, wouldn't give up the fight
Couldn't tell from her smile but she'd seen hell
They compared scars, talked battle up til night
She's The Purple Rose, just Rose for this tale
Fight was not hers, so she refused to fall
Said she'd seen too much to tell it all.

IV

The tale of Rose is not from fresh new fruit
Rose was not prepared for the tears she wept
Winds of life blows on us all, same ol root
Her first wind left Rose feeling low and swept
She recalls praying for a man who knew

She thought she could love enough to withstand
If God is love, then she ignored the cue
She didn't know she was afoot hot sand
Fugitived and charred was Rose's young life
Eschewed patience, she rushed in way too soon
All she wanted: to be a loving wife
The Scorpion made Rose sing a new tune
A winded tune she'd learn to sing too well
Pierced heart, ripped, cowed, it was hopeless to tell.

V

Their first conversation went much like this
"I am a passionate man and so then,
I need a passionate woman." Sealed kiss.
What he really meant. "My emotions send
me in a rage because of jealous eyes."
Beat down by his tongue made a useless pulp
Maya Angelou's words rang: "Still I Rise"
Rose could not rise, pill too big to gulp
No healing rang from the reviling tongue
It lashed, it hurt, it pierced, cut Rose deep
It stenched of pure dung and skillfully sung
She aversely sat in his darkened creep
Terrorized and crushed and all the time
Who could Rose tell of this heinous crime?

VI

Sold Rose the dream while her eyes were still fixed
Calumnied, maligned, abated, shamed

196

Rose felt like it was her mind playing tricks
Sang hatred and anger with eyes inflamed
Sang praises at sometimes so proud and great
Bewildered, perplexed, confusing as heck
Up and down, off and on, love and hate; wait
Rose pondered trying to ring her own neck
Trained to doubt her own sanity and mind
Set up, crippled, yearning for what's less hot
Accused then praised, cussed out then spoke to kind
Sometimes in front of others sometimes not
Not certain whether she should smile or cry
Thinking about a way to say goodbye.

VII

Not barefoot she was pregnant as always
Incapacitated by her nurture.
Tried to do the right thing bearing his ways:
Criticized lame, crushed; and freedom searched her.
Fell to the floor to cry out to God, please
She cried for many years with a sad face
Her recourse was simply, drop to torn knees
Disregarded wedded wife was her place
She glimpsed "Rose" from the mirror on the wall
Hidden behind the aging, frowned, sad she
She heard a faint distressing inner call
Look, wake up, and open your eyes, it's me
Gather your little ones, now, they need hope
Otherwise, they will never learn to cope.

VIII

Startled and shaken by light she could see
She vaguely recalled the years that slipped by
Gone was her sunshine, yet she chose to flee
When her first-borns moaned, wept, and when they cried
Finally, opening her tear stained eyes
Each had scars in dire need of mending
Rose could now hear her children's private cries
Waiting for her to see to their tending
The beatings her son received must now end
Her daughter's beatdowns must come to a halt
She knew well his pride wouldn't let him bend
Watching, children will be what they are taught
She had to make a clear choice for her lot
It was time to leap from the seething pot.

IX

She pleaded to God like never before
Afraid of God's eternal burning flame
While making plans to let butt hit the door
Transforming strength now burned within her frame.
We have all fallen short of God's glory
Who can stand in time of His great coming?
Rose can testify of her grim story
Amid fear, relief, freedom succumbing.
She had no idea what she would now do
Though she knew to keep her eyes rooted up
No mercy though worship family knew

Prayed for strength to carry this bitter cup
Shaky and scared, she gathered strength to pack
Teared Rose did not want to ever go back.

X

Rose didn't want to go back to devil's spell
"You are trifling, I don't want you now?"
"You are stupid," Rose dared go against hell
"You are a whore," "Whose baby is it now?"
"You have no virtue," he would yell and yell
"You are a good wife," then "why did I vow?"
"You are my love," then "foolish slut," Rose fell
Hit bang slam bleeding heart hurt bend and bow
"Please don't send me back to revile and rail"
"Oh God please how much more will you allow?"
Why was she alone lonely in a jail?
How could she break this wrong and ugly vow?
Caress or curse fond loath love or hate rap?
Rejected or protected kiss or slap?

XI

Rose had no warning what more could have come
No one could have paid her a million bucks
Stony hearted him made her heart beat numb
Ignoring his seed evidenced pure nuts
His rejection heightened their acute scars
Here lies a Bible teaching infidel
Worse thing she had seen in this curse by far

But she too was a sinner who could fail
Reflecting back on what has now gone past
On his sin, she should not have fixed her eyes
Serpent lurched a trick he leeched on her fast
Tumultuous wind: near loss of the prize
Lil Big Man, tempest winds for short while
Fabricated a lie that stole her smile.

XII

Contrived, simulation of a best friend
Skillful deception and again Rose cried
From pillow to pillow, floor to floor, and den to den
She contemplated doom because he lied
She was not supposed to be his secret
Rejection sourced all of her inbred fears
He tried to alter that for which she was meant
Cut as deep as the first winds years of tears
Naivete was an enemy to Rose
Imagine if you dare, your heart ripped out
This describes pain that would curl up her toes
Acute, severe suffering, darkened doubt
Jesus stepped in before her breath took flight
Sent prayer, praise, Bible, pen, and his might.

XIII

What happened to her Sisters in Prayer?
Cunning women of prayer were not there
The winds abandoned her as she stood frayed

Deliverance vow broken as they stare
Repulsion and abandonment held fast
Shadowed pain bitterly through day and night
Left alone to taste torment hardly cast
She was tossed, wound up and bound very tight
But it was the fault of this tainted Rose
Since Jesus gave already instructions
Bitterness hovered her heart, that slammed close
God said, "trust no man", nor their seductions
Man is both male and friend fickle female
Rose quenched a shout, "All 'yall go straight to hell!

XIV

Nevertheless, words for Rose wisped trust God
Bid care to male or female so freely
Refrain fluent voice bench tranquilly nod
Heart and mind belong to no one but He
Word taught to forgive for forgiveness sake
She had nothing to hold against others
She wanted no part of the hot filled lake
Wished well to all the sisters and brothers
Alone yet full with hope, she can now live
Mending the tears in her heart which she bare
Not everyone knows how to love nor give
Neither angry nor bitter; Rose can't care
Erasing the shadowy tears of fear
Refined, awaiting her time and her year.

XV

This almost ends her saga for just now
Empowered by a makeover of mind
More winds might blow her way as Rose learns how
To let lose tainted dreams poorly designed
Each frustration brings a different sort
Of challenge rage tragedy utter loss
Preparation for judgement at last court
Some speak of boll weevils, rain, draught, or moss
All touched by beauty and some classed by fame
Some speak in sonnet, ballad, or free verse
All will have to bow to God's mighty name
Life is given to practice and rehearse
Rose is no exception to this great plan
Same question; "Who shall be able to stand?"

XVI

Sister Care Too Much has since gone and split
Sister Called Hurt left just the other day
Rose had no mind to really notice it
Sister Anger was not the last to stay
Sister Self Pity grieved Lil Big Man
Inhaled deeply she tried hard to let go
He was supposed to ask her for her hand
Bruised gash lingered dense til Rose avowed, "NO!"
Rose solely thought of the Scorpion when
Matters of the children came to her mind
His seed she will forever have to tend

202

Otherwise he is pushed back far behind
Rose and she are one, we talk the same talk
She is Rose's mirror; Rose is her walk.

XVII

Emotional abstinence, pleasant calm
Uncomplaining of circumstances bound
Cool. Using the Word as her soothing balm
Quiet. Not uttering a single sound
Temperately bearing the inertia
Repress the pain of annoying hardship
Indifferent to life's militia
Consciously letting God steer the big ship
Song of hope long: walking through the twelve gates
Song of joy dance: giving Him constant praise
Song of peace be still: she quietly waits
Song of virtue strong: through tumult and maze
Fruited from The Purple Rose: meet patience,
Having her perfect work, experience.

www.ingramcontent.com/pod-product-compliance
Lightning Source LLC
Chambersburg PA
CBHW030523020726
47494CB00004B/1215